BERYL GILROY was born in Guyana and came to England in 1951. Though an experienced teacher, she was forced to take jobs as a clerk and a domestic – including a spell in an old people's home – before being able to resume her career in education. This has involved teaching, researching, lecturing and the headship of a London primary school. She now works as a Counselling Psychologist, and holds a PhD in that discipline.

Between 1970 and 1975 she wrote a series of children's books (Macmillan), and in 1976 she published *Black Teacher* (Cassell), the chronicle of her experiences as the only Black headmistress in her London Borough. In 1982 she won the GLC Creative Writing Ethnic Minorities Prize with *In For A Penny* (Holt Saunders), and in 1985 her novel, *Frangipani House* (Heinemann), won a prize in the GLC Black Literature Competition.

BERYL GILROY

BOY-SANDWICH

HEINEMANN

Heinemann Educational Publishers
A division of Heinemann Publishers (Oxford) Ltd
Halley Court, Jordan Hill, Oxford OX2 8EJ

Heinemann: A division of Reed Publishing (USA) Inc.
361 Hanover Street, Portsmouth, NH 03801-3912, USA

Heinemann Educational Books (Nigeria) Ltd
PMB 5205, Ibadan
Heinemann Educational Boleswa
PO Box 10103, Village Post Office, Gaborone, Botswana

FLORENCE   PRAGUE   PARIS   MADRID
ATHENS   MELBOURNE   JOHANNESBURG
AUCKLAND   SINGAPORE   TOKYO
CHICAGO   SAO PAULO

First published by Heinemann International in the
Caribbean Writers Series in 1989

British Library Cataloguing in Publication Data

Gilroy, Beryl
Boy-sandwich.
I. Title   II. Series
813 [F]

ISBN 0-435-98810-7

Photoset by Wilmaset, Birkenhead, Wirral
Printed and bound in Great Britain by
Cox & Wyman Ltd, Reading, Berkshire

94 95 96 10 9 8 7 6 5 4 3

In loving memory of
Pat Gilroy (1919–1975)
and Uncle George (1890–1979)

To Jagdish, Bev and Mike, who gave me space to write this book.
To the many elderly West Indians to whom I talked and to the founder
members of the Camden Black Sisters' Beryl Gilroy Library who spoke
with me and discussed the dialogue in this book.

B. G.

AUTHOR'S NOTE

This story is based on many true incidents, particularly those in the life of my husband's Uncle George, who spent his last days in a home for the elderly at London's Branch Hill. This home was investigated by the local authority and exposed for cruelty to the residents. It has subsequently been closed down.

CHAPTER ONE

That morning stubborn clouds hung low and brought feelings I could describe only as irregular. It seemed as if time itself was being agitated, the echoes of the past colliding with the voices of the present, creating moments that boiled and swirled and pushed. I drove fast, much too fast for that time of day. Speed, I thought, was the answer to the turbulence and frustration inside me.

A road sweeper, struggling to subdue the chaotic borders of debris, leaned on his broom and crossed himself as I drove by. I imagined myself pursuing a point of moving light imprisoned in a tunnel. It challenged me and compelled me to move forward, unconcerned for my own safety or for that of my parents, who sat tense and nervous in the back seat of my car.

'Don't drive so crazy', snapped my mother. 'We want to arrive in one piece.' Ignoring her remark, I turned into Selwyn Avenue where my grandparents had lived for many years.

The house in that once unsavoury part of London was theirs. For years they had tended it and cared for the garden with a love that was deep and eloquent. The kind of love one gave to a helpless child. Now the developers had won their way. The old couple were being forced to accept the pittance offered for their home so that it could lawfully be demolished, along with others, to make room for town houses which only the rich could afford. My grandparents had held out for as long as they could but time had run out. The day for eviction had arrived and they were about to embark on the journey which some old folk sometimes must make – the journey to the limbo of a sheltered home.

As we approached my grandparents' house the silence suddenly snapped. The house itself had lost its well-cared-for look and dust from the rubble of the surrounding construction work had formed a film on the windows; but my grandparents could be seen from the outside like two ghostly figures. Voices of idle onlookers seeking early-morning distraction rose and fell, while rent-a-mob racists stood around.

Clutching their Union Jacks, they thumped their chests as they chanted, 'Nigs out!' 'Schwartzers out!' We stopped close to the front door. The racists booed and held their flags high. My grandparents, dressed and waiting, had heard it all before. Those days would never return but they would always live in memory.

My grandpa hurried to the lavatory and then, hand in hand, he and my grandmother walked regally round the room, stroking and caressing the walls in a final goodbye. There was an upsurge of chanting as they opened the front door but the rumble of the bulldozers getting into position drowned out the voices. Our few supporters could only stare helplessly at those faces so welcoming of the chaos around them.

The police arrived, crossed the road and reprimanded the racists. It made things worse. Sergeant Keeler, whom I knew, walked round the garden. He recognised me. When I was twelve, and he a policeman on the beat, he used to sus-search* me every single day just for fun.

'No more wogs! Out! Out! Out!' came lovelessly to our ears. A brief smile played round the sergeant's lips as the racists yelled. The whole performance was funny enough for tears.

'You must leave, Mr Grainger,' said the sergeant. 'You've made your point. You're an old man.'

'Tell those racist cowards!' shouted my father. 'Not us! The old people are where they belong!'

'You may not like what they're saying but free speech is what we British are all about,' he replied. 'I would advise you to help your parents and conclude this unpleasant business.'

*sus-search: search on suspicion.

2

'Harassment!' yelled my mother. 'Injustice!' It did not take much to whip up a storm inside her.

'Persecution in de name of de Union Jack,' Grandma chimed in. 'Ever seen such a t'ing!'

More chants of 'Nigs out!' 'Schwartzers out!' came at us like bricks.

'Mr Grainger,' said another policeman. 'Please, sir, let's go. It's the best thing to do.' He curled an arm round Grandpa's shoulder. 'This is a building site now, sir.'

'Don't touch him!' yelled my mother. 'He's not a person in your world! Get off him!'

As I looked out, I could see a priest trying to reason with the racists.

'Calm and peace,' said my grandpa. 'De Lord save Daniel from de jaws of death. God will protect us.'

'Make sure you have everything,' I said. 'This is the point of no return. These are people, not lions. A small part of a large population.'

We walked cautiously out of the house and entered the car, but before we could drive off a small group of militants encircled us, banging on the roof and rocking the car. Grandpa wet himself. My dad began to wheeze. The police waded in, using their truncheons liberally. My mum screamed. Grandma became hysterical.

'Don't hit us!' the mob yelled. 'Hit them!'

The police, still wielding truncheons, cleared a path for us and I accelerated to safety. A few yards away I stopped the car and reassured my family. Some of our supporters had followed us to offer help.

My grandparents were softly crying – it was as if they were singing a very sad song about their fears and the noises that now echoed in their heads.

'Don't cry,' I said. 'Everything will be OK. Racists hunt in packs – like wolves.'

I talked to them, the way my mum had often talked to me. Grandpa nodded. He stared out of the window as if his eyes were making contact with something unrelated to the present. He tried to talk but the words he wanted to speak had been swallowed. We changed his trousers in the car and he didn't like that kind of invasion of his privacy at all. After several more stops for reassurance we arrived at the sheltered accommodation which the social worker had recommended. The Birches offered communal facilities, allowed personal possessions and admitted people of all races. We were not entirely happy to leave my grandparents but I reckoned I would be around to see fair play. I promised myself that, come what may, the year before my university course began was theirs. I was going to live to be a hundred. What was one single year in a giant life-span like that?

My grandparents are the only couple of West Indian origin in the home, with the exception of Belladora, a woman of mixed race who would change anything that would 'guarantee the extraction of coloured blood from my veins!'. Those are her own words, but they wash over my grandparents, who are worried about what they have chosen, and are even more concerned about how they are going to come to terms with living in a crowd and obeying the rules while unable to cook the food they like. I promise to seek out a supply of colourless blood for Belladora but she ignores my remark and glares at me as if I were a crap-and-concrete construction.

The family hangs around for a while after the old people have been admitted. My father, who has been in hospital himself with ulcers and asthma, is in tears. 'I feel so guilty. I'm their only son and I can't do better than this for them. They should be going home to live and die in peace among their own.'

'It's not their "own" now, Robby,' my mother says bitterly. 'They been in this country long, paid their taxes, did dog-work. Blood, sweat and tears! England owe it to them!'

My mother finally calms down, fitting their experience to her years in Britain. 'Things will work out.'

Grandma has found an armchair and sat down in it.

'Get up, get up,' snaps Belladora. 'That's my chair!'

'Show us all you chairs, frontish woman,' snaps back Grandpa. 'Every chair in here is you own?'

'I guess you want two chairs side by side, Mr Grainger,' the

4

Matron asks pleasantly. She is a white woman in whose voice I recognise a hint of Jamaica. 'Here you are.'

She leads them to two contrasting armchairs, one with pale yellow velvet upholstery, the other tacky and ancient. Grandpa sits down. A smile scurries across his face. 'It feel nice,' he says. He has met his chair, a worn-out faded chair, with a stubbornness that matches his own. It seems to resent those who must sit upon it. Little thorns of horsehair push their way out of the upholstery as if trying to reach the light. The wooden arms have become worn and smooth over time since the hands of the elderly are inept and cannot vandalise property. I look at my grandparents sitting as if they have come to the end of a long, rough road with their youth in the distance and their yesterdays wrapped about them like a well-worn blanket. They show all the signs of old age: the weakness, the incipient tiredness and most of all the surrender to the will of others.

Grandpa always loved to talk but today he is so silent! Now and then – and only now and then – there are glimpses of his spirit. All through my youth and in the early days of his retirement, he had talked to me about times long since gone and had pointed out friends and family in the album to prove the more important points of argument and reason. It is the most treasured of his possessions – this album of pages overburdened with photographs. Some are so faded they are hardly discernible. Others are the colour of sepia-brown earth. In a voice marked with the twang of his Island he would often talk of those yesterdays when he kept his many assignations with destiny, across seas and oceans and in the countries beyond.

Today he is a resident of a sheltered home with his wife because his son could not arrange things otherwise. I, his only grandson, whisper, 'Grampa and Gran, I'll come back and we'll talk. Remember how we used to talk?' They both smile and nod. Amid this feeling of betrayal I recall Grandpa's testimony of self. He talked about himself with such certainty! He once told me of his humble beginnings.

He said, 'Tyrone, if I tell you where I come from, you would know where you must go. I come from a goodly family, you

5

know, and a goodly, Christian home. Every Sunday, come rain come shine, we go to church to praise our God!'

He said, 'our God' as if this person was an old familiar friend who knew him even before he was born.

'I never live with my mother and father. I give to a barren aunt to keep her from grievin' for children that never come to her. My father is her brother. He have five and he keep four. Two and two, and give her de odd one, me. I ent odd in dat sense. I am de odd number – number three.

'My Auntie Dora live on de sugar estate wid her husband, uncle Dandeau Clark. She is a kind woman, quiet and deep as a gubby* to strangers but lovin' and givin' to family, especially to her husband, although as things prove he didn't worth it. Dey live on de estate in a long row-house or range, what dey call terrace here – a little two-room place wid it own doorstep for family and friends to sit on in de evenin' when work is done. Dey have de bedroom and I sleep in a cot in de front room. My aunt use to tease me, say, "If t'ief man come you is de first dey will tek."

'Uncle Dandeau have a hawkish face wid his eye fix on you. He don't like cane-work but in dem days dere is no choice for no one. Every afternoon we look out for him. If he don't come by lamp-light, Auntie Dora crawl de room wid worry. Her spirit, mind, heart and soul like a stormy ocean till she see him. When she see him, she wave her hand sof'ly, like she dustin' de air, and a smile would come like a light between dem, and her eyes would twinkle wid happiness so dey look like two stars in de darkness of her face.

'My job is to soak Uncle foot in lukewarm salt-water to refresh de bruise on dem and cure dem. And when de water swallow his foot he give out a long sigh that come from deep inside his soul and he thank God for a child though not his own, for Auntie Dora and for warm salt-water. Den we sit down to eat simple food – yam, rice, salt-fish, manioc, simple food, cook wid love and cook careful. I use to notice Uncle Dandeau teeth. Dey use to move sudden and when he waitin' for food, dey use to raise up. At dat

*gubby: gourd from calabash tree.

6

time I never know 'bout false teeth. I use to 'fraid for his teeth, den one day he show me, and I ent 'fraid for dem no more.

'My Auntie Dora is a woman of grace – graceful like a palm leaf in a mild breeze – gentle of looks and fair of face. On Sunday, dress up in her skirt and silk shawl she buy at the Estate sale, she move like de queen although her husband cut cane. She use to sing wid a voice as sweet as mother milk. I know of baby to stop cryin' when she sing, and dyin' people to leave dis world peaceful and rich from her singin'. She herself die when I twelve years old. Her husband cry and bawl and throw himself about. For three days he lie down in a hammock like a dead fish, cryin' and moanin' for her. Everybody tendin' to him, helpin' him to bear it. Den what he do? 'He marry a Rosehall woman – four month after! Dat false-face man! When we confront him wid his deeds he say, 'God give Eve unto Adam and besides, Dora it was dat tell me to married down Rosehall way if she ever die.'

'And after de funeral he say he dream dat "Dora appear in de form of a child and lead him to de said woman house"! We have to believe him because nobody ever tek notice of dat particular woman before. She use to dance for her livin'. She learn people to dance waltz and t'ing, and she take Uncle Dandeau out of de cane wid de money dey pay her.

'My Auntie Dora very strict wid me. See her here!' He pointed to the picture of her standing by her door. 'She was my mother, my sister, my auntie, my friend, all good relative for a man to have.'

From the photograph Auntie Dora is tall and hipsy with brushed-back hair. Her clothes are simple. Her hands are purposeful and strong. She is in control of her smile.

'Why do you say she was strict, Grandpa?' I asked.

'Now, now, don't get de wrong end. I ent mean slave-driver strict. I mean strict as a good mother. Tek dat one and only time I gamble! She use to bake bread every Friday and I sell de bread from door to door for cash money. One day I collect up four dollar, and happy as a monkey wid a bunch of bananas I goin' home. Well, I have to pass through an alley and right at de end of de alley is a rowdy crowd round a man sittin' front of a cloth

7

spread flat. In front of him is three coconut shell, smooth and painted white. He playin' "bet and win" wid de coconut shell and a pigeon-pea seed. "Put down you money where you t'ink de peas settle. Bet and win," he bawl out, like a money shark. You can tell by de way he shoutin'. Like he in trouble and he hollerin' for help.

'Everybody laughin' and arguin'. Not a soul doin'. He slick as slime with de coconut shell, but he don't bargain for young eyes like mine! De youngness of my eye help me and I begin to see de seed. De devil whisperin' me all de time and it just like I can see de seed through de shell. Suddenly de devil move me to action and I slam down de four dollar in front of a particular shell, like it is a domino and bound to be winner of de game. De man start to move de cup again.

' "No!" everybody shout. "Fair play! Hoist up de shell! Hoist it up! De money put down!" Reluctantly, de man hoist up de shell and dere before man and God is de peas – little, round and brown as dry-wood. I win another four dollar – me! A little boy wid all dat money! De crowd glad de man lose and dey start followin' me home, clappin' and laughin' and shoutin' like dey practisin' for a fête-and-dance. When we reach de house de noise bring Auntie Dora to de door-mouth. Axe set down in front of her and arms akimbo, she settle to defend me. She t'ink I do something needin' correction and she not takin' it to heart till she hear my version of de ruction. Shameface, I tell her de story and give her de money.

' "You gamble?" she ask quietly.

' "Yes, Auntie Dora."

' "You ever see me or you Uncle Dan gamble?"

' "No, Auntie Dora."

' "You ever see you father or mother gamble?"

'I shake my head.

' "Den where you get gamble from ? "

' "I don't know."

' "Well, I goin' lick it out of you. Give me a belt, somebody!" De same man wid de money, quick as a fly, pull out his belt an hand it to my aunt. He have a sudden wish to spite me and hear me holler.

'She lash me from head to foot. Every time she lash, she shout, "Don't gamble, you hear me!" Through my tears I have to reassure her dat never again would I do such a t'ing. I never gamble from dat day to dis. She burn de money in front of everybody. "I don't want gamble money in my house. I poor but never sinful," she say. People learn a lesson that day. Dey never see such a woman like my Auntie Dora. From dat day to dis!'

She was a woman of yesterday, as Grandpa's sisters Drusylla and Carrie were. I once asked about them and Grandpa said, 'Dey was two ugly sisters – ugly in character. Drusylla younger dan me, was hard-face wid a tongue so sharp you could skin a shark wid it. She use to call me "Cane-Man", say I live in de canefield like a duppee* and she use to drag me off de chair. She say I use to floor-sittin'. Carrie use to copy her. She a preacher prayin' for her own soul. Before she turn to preachin' she sell in de market. It hard for her. She married two or tree time but it don't leave a print on her. She barren like Auntie Dora and now she preachin' and livin' down by Coral Rock Bay last time I hear.'

Today my eyes wander around this room where there is dust as thick as paste on the pictures hanging on the wall. The old people are silent, curled around their pasts and their thoughts. The Matron and her caregivers are working hard to reassure us by their actions and presence. My parents are still trying to decide whether there is time to reconsider and find different solutions to this problem of ageing relatives.

'Let's all give this a try,' I suggest. 'Let's see what happens. I can deal with officialdom – besides, they can always go home. Home to us, I mean. I'll help. I'll always help.'

Then I say again, 'Goodbye, Grandpa, goodbye, Gran, I'll come tomorrow.'

My love for my grandparents fills me to the brim. I am happy to help them settle into a life among strangers. I wish I had a

duppee: Spirit of a dead person.

magic wand with which I could wave their fears away, but life is never enchanted. Life has sharp teeth and sharper claws. I wave. They wave back. I wave again. They are by now talking animatedly to the woman beside them. They seem to have settled in.

CHAPTER TWO

Today Grandma is in her chair. She is clutching her bag, which is stuffed like a pregnant capybara with her possessions. Her bag contains the things she vows no one but me would inherit after her death. It's no use saying I don't want them. They are mostly the tools of her trade – thimbles of all sizes, pinking shears, scissors, tape-measures, boxes of pins, scraps of jewellery and her money. She talks of her doubloons, though no one has ever seen them. As far as money goes, there are small plastic bags with a few coins – some old and strange and some she says her father gave her years ago. There is also a pair of shoes she wore to a dance in 1952. The West Indian dance was held at a church hall in Brixton.

'De dance end at ten o'clock but everybody happy,' she confided the day she showed me the shoes. 'De police shut down de dance. Say it noisy and workin' people want sleep. In dem days dey say black people tek social security more dan white people, same as dey do today.'

In her Island home she had danced as well, and had kept Grandpa Simon interested in her by refusing him a waltz when she observed his antics with his cousin Julinda. She continued to ignore him until he promised to give up slaving for his father for little reward. Under her supervision he abandoned tailoring and joined his brothers who were at that time running contraband between the islands. When the adventurers returned they brought money and trinkets which made girls cluster round them. They went dancing, drank rum, made babies and played dominoes. But Simon's heart was not in it. He married Grandma and took up tailoring again, but this time in partnership with his

11

father. His mother welcomed Clara Riley. She was known to have a good character and understood all the fine points of etiquette. She was no pick-head shrimp of a girl. Happy with her husband, she continued dressmaking until her fate brought her to London. My father was a sickly child and so fearing that the cold weather would cause his kind of blood to congeal, Grandma left him with her parents and her sister until the roots of life had grown deeply into his body. That took seventeen years. Fate never allowed her to indulge her only son, so Grandma belonged to me. I was her baby. She loved me and looked after me.

When she met me from school and took me home to tea, I felt a deep pleasure. The colours of the fabrics piled up everywhere in her rooms made me pretend I was in some rainbow country that I had conquered. Grandma would let me feel the silks, the satins, the cottons and the crêpes and she would tell me their names; and when Grandpa came in from the garden we would take tea together. He always drank maté while we drank chocolate sent from home. It was real chocolate – made from cocoa beans, sun-dried, roasted and ground. It had no additives and no sugar. It flowed through those who drank it in a wave of heat, and Gran said the sweating it caused cleansed the body.

Today there is another kind of teatime. There is the clanking and shivering of crockery. A trolley is being wheeled in by a plump, inscrutable girl. Her hair – half-red, half-black – is piled on her head and a little cap is perched on the very top. The clanking goes on for ages before the trolley reaches my grand-parents. Grandpa sips his tea and, as I watch, I recall my grandmother officiating at our tea-table, her hair in neat clumps, her apron lily-white. There is a picture of the teapot in the album. It is old and large and strange. Gran had difficulty lifting it when it was full. She served us cuts of her special chocolate and vanilla cake. She served us patties of pastry filled with succulent minced meat. For extras there were pineapple tartlets and homemade ginger-beer.

Today the trolley stops beside the aged, the infirm. Cups of the panacea are handed round this lifeless room full of dying life. The caregiver smiles superciliously and wheedles in the voice she

12

keeps especially for the old people. She dredges up a highpitched sound and puts a few words to it.

'Alice, milk and two sugars, for you, Alice? There's a good girl.'

'Don't call me girl! You're the girl! I am the woman. I married three times. All my children conceived in a wedding bed,' Alice retorts angrily. Alice is a sleeping terrier who will bite and tear anyone to death.

'Never mind that, dear. Here's your tea.' Alice moves forward, grasps a sticky cake and drops it into her cup.

'No, not with that, Alice. Not with that! *Stir it*, dear! Not with the cake! The *spoon! The spoon!*'

There is a note of despair in the caregiver's voice and she turns to Grandma.

'Put down your bag, Clara. You can't hold a large bag, a small bag and a cup of tea. You haven't got three hands, have you, dear.'

I reach for the small bag Gran is holding. It is a linen bag full of Island earth, which she brought with her and has always kept with her. It is as sacred as her cross and her Bible. Did not the book say, 'Dust thou art, and unto dust shalt thou return'? One day earth would cover her lifeless body and this special earth would lie beside her in her box (her favourite word for coffin).

Gran has wandered off without her cup of tea rather than be parted from her possessions. She loathes any contact with this caregiver but she conceals her loathing. Instead she is silent. She is a child again, to be seen and not heard.

Her voice is her most personal possession but, like a tap that has been turned off, she has been silenced by the unyielding routine of things and she disappears into her room where I follow her. There is an overwhelming smell of decay. Without much effort, I discover the source – the bowl of fruit on the table. The oranges are rotten and ageing, the apples grub-infested. The bananas look like fingers covered with large neglected sores. I peer into the half-open drawer of their dressing-table. That too is full of rotten food – bits of cheese, ancient slices of fruitcake and chopped-up corned beef and Spam. It is a nauseating sight and I empty everything into the bin and take it downstairs. I inform the caregiver of my find but she ignores me, smiles sweetly and says, 'Not a bit of trouble, those two. They never say a word. They've got an album with some nice old pictures. I can get a good price for them – especially the ones with black people dressed up like Victorians. They must have been going out to a fancy-dress ball. Blacks are mostly naked. Aren't they?'

I wonder why the fact that she is talking about my great-grandparents has escaped her. I decide to take the album under my care so that she would not get to the photographs even to show them to an honest priest.

Grandpa has complained that some of his clothes are missing. I enquire about them and am told that they are being cleaned. Belladora announces that some of the inmates' clothes are taken out and sold, and as a precaution I make an inventory of Grandpa's things, since men's clothes tend to disappear most of all. My grandpa always made himself beautiful shirts and suits; he was always immaculately dressed. He imitated his father, dressing like him on Sundays and striving after his respectability. All the family dressed in an 'uptown' way. My brother Goldberg had learnt to stitch early and had made his own clothes at an age when other children played cowboys.

The only time Grandpa had difficulty getting materials to work with was during the war, but he dyed his own cotton and sold homemade shirts. His one indulgence was his camera. He was fond of photography and took many pictures, keeping them in the album – which now serves as a beacon to his past. As children we were not allowed unsupervised access to either his camera or his album. Grandpa kept his album all through the war and through the hurricanes which from time to time visited the Island.

The war brought problems to the Island. Men and women enlisted in their thousands to fight the Germans. Grandpa's brothers, Tomas and Daniel, hid themselves in Venezuela and Grandpa was compelled to stay at home and provide for his parents. Meanwhile my father was born. Times were hard and hard times, like a disease, plagued everyone on the Island.

Grandpa said. 'Everybody pray for de war to end and for England to win. Dey show films of what will happen if de Germans win. Slavery will come back, so fear is like solid rock inside people's hearts. Trade start to suffer and de price of food reach rock-bottom. When de war at last is at an end dere is processions, prayer-meetin's and dances but dere is also deep sorrow for England, our mother-country, for everyt'ing she go through. However, people still hanker after America. People flock from all over de world to America and it make t'ings difficult for us, de black Island-people, to get dere. It a plain case of keep de black man out wherever you turn.

'But the hurricane change everyt'ing. We use to know when de rainy season comin' and when de dry season start. Everyt'ing is cut-out, crystal clear. Den everyt'ing change. De weather get topsy-turvy and de hurricane come.'

Grandma took up the story.

One day 'bout two o'clock, afternoon time, when de sun ujually hot, you know, full heat, de sky turn a dark syrupy molasses black. Minutes pass and de raindrop begin hammer down and turn everyt'ing to mud and hog-wash. It trubulent outside and you can almost cut de heat like you cut a cake. Next day hot weather 'gain. De sky burn and shrivel up whatever green, whatever flourishin' and whatever obtain substance from de bosom of de earth. We expect a hurricane but it never come. Den de next week de hurricane come. First, we hear a sound like devils callin'. A long, long knot-up chord of sound comin' fast and furious towards everyt'ing and every mortal man. Wid dat sound wonderment and terror come and tek you over, and all you can do is fall on you knees whether you on grass or ground and pray for strength to face it and meet it eye to eye.'

'Is de thunder dat frighten me,' Grandpa said. 'It rattle like a million maracas in de hands of dem dat is stronger dan iron, stronger dan stone. Lightnin', fiery yellow lightnin', make a map of de skies and de wind begin to howl and scream and put out strong arms dat snatch up and throw everyt'ing before it.

Everyt'ing flyin' about in de air like de devil and his army tearin' up hell, and den lettin' t'ings fall sprawlin' over people. De wind rake up de canes, tumblin' and whippin' dem as if dey is dry grass. Our genip tree – a child to us – turn upside-down, de root of it like a man wid small head and heavy dreadlocks. It lie down on de road wid a mighty crash. When three hours pass, de storm die down and one by one people begin to crawl out from underneath destruction. De livin' help de dead but confusion tek over. House smash up 'gainst trees, donkey-cart where you never t'ink a donkey-cart would ever go, and everywhere motherless children yellin' and shoutin'.

'Mercifully we safe. But everybody cry and we cry too. De wind blow away de top half of our house and leave de other half. It hold strong. It never fall on top of us. Me and some other men offer words of consolation and when day dawn de full damage is frightenin'.

'People come in to help us. Blankets, food and medicine come in. We bury our dead and start to build anew. "Let us start at once, never give up!" I shout. And everybody follow my shoutin' wid dey own. Every hole and corner put to use but life never de same 'gain. People refuse to trust nature and dey start to look round for a safe place to go and live. I hold on for 'bout ten month den a man come from England to recruit people to work in hospitals, London Transport and British Railways. I get a job as assistant recruitin' officer and de first person I recruit is me! I recruit me, Simon Grainger, to work for England. But all dat happen yesterday – a long time ago.'

There's a picture of Grandpa sitting at a table under a tree in the company of a white man wearing a topee. An umbrella is providing additional protection from the sun for the white man. There is a line of men waiting to be interviewed. In spite of the searing heat, they all have their hats in their hands. Grandpa called such actions 'being mannersable'. It is a favourite word of his, and he says it with a touch of deference in his voice.

Today he looks perplexed. He ignores the album. He seems to be overwhelmed with thoughts that make him unable to cope. There are tears in his eyes.

16

'Give Juney a five pound,' he says. 'If I have my pension I would pay. What happen to my pension book? I never have money. Clara leave in de bath too long. She cold. I try to take her out but I couldn't and Belladora went out so no one give me a hand. You must give Juney five pound to help us. Everybody payin' Juney. If you don't pay you get by-pass. They leave you sittin' in de water till dey done watchin' television, *Coronation Street*. When I ask for money, dey give me fifty pence.'

I have asked repeatedly about my gandparents' pension but the replies are always vague. In fact I am regarded as a 'bolshie black' since Grandpa, I am so often told, is able to manage his own affairs. Today, outraged, I go in search of the caregiver called Juney. She is hard to find. I follow the sound of voices and find them all in a room tucked away out of sight from the hall. They are sitting round bottles of Frascati and there are glasses and paper cups on the table.

'There you all are,' I say. 'Two things. I want a drink for my gran to take her pills with and I want to know who is Juney?' I have done the unthinkable and ignored the STAFF ONLY sign on the door.

'Who is Juney?' I ask again.

'Me,' says a drink-soaked voice. I catch sight of a plump red-eyed woman in a plain off-white overall, a roll of fat in the path of the sleeve like a wedge.

'Why have you to be paid five pounds?' I ask, hurling the words at her.

'Five pounds! What five pounds?' She is surly at being found out.

'That my grandfather insisted you must be paid to take my grandmother out of the bath. Isn't that your job?'

'That old besom is talking out of his messy arse,' she says in a drunken snarl. 'I'll . . .'

'You'll do what?' I snarl back. 'Touch them and there will be blood and guts all over the place. I am on to your little game. Like hell, you're being good to old people. Sucking their blood like vampires!'

Later I am sent a letter by the Matron objecting to the length of my visits. In my reply I explain that my people and I spend our time in the bar, the lounge and on a seat in the garden, weather permitting. I will always visit and stay as long as I like until I go to university. I explain that had I a choice I myself would take care of my grandparents who had once been employed taxpayers.

I report The Birches to the town hall. But at the town hall no one really knows how the homes are run. They have every confidence in the staff, they tell me. The town hall is in fact afraid of the unions. A strike would be called and thousands of old people would suffer. Grandpa and Grandma are expendable. Two old people don't really count.

I look at their wedding photo. It is faded and Grandma's features are hardly discernible. She is sitting and Grandpa is standing behind her. I wonder if they ever thought their days would end like this. Did they imagine a brood of children and then manage only one, who was too riddled with asthma to visit? I daren't tell my mother of Grandpa's insistence on paying June, about the staff's drinking and their obvious neglect of the old people. My mother is not discreet and Grandpa and Gran are at the mercy of these people. I try to see the Matron but she is away for a few days. At least, that's what I'm told. Later I notice the Assistant Matron talking to a man in the back garden.

Knowing how possessions have 'disappeared', I suspect the man is an antique dealer and a fence. The conversation floats on a stream of laughter and camaraderie. I stand where I could be seen.

'Buying, selling or barter?' I ask.

They try to scare me with curled lips and fierce glances, but I stand my ground and the Assistant Matron rapidly disappears. To the dealer, however, I am just a London black, dreadlocked, feckless and looking for trouble, and 'should be sent back with my spliffs to God knows where'.

I decide to take whatever valuables Grandma has to my home for safe keeping. But already her watch has disappeared. No one has seen it.

'Did she have a watch?' every caregiver asks, faking concern.

'Fancy her having a watch! I would have thought telling the time was beyond Clara.'

That is all I can get in answer to any question about Grandma's dear old watch!

CHAPTER THREE

When Grandpa arrived in Britain, a black master tailor was unheard of and so he worked as a garage hand in London Transport's Willesden Garage. In the album he seems happy enough although he knows he is cut off from any of the worthwhile areas of British life. Funnily enough, he and his mates are all smoking cigars and smiling. They stand in groups of white and black people, looking cross-eyed at each other.

'I celebratin' de arrival of my first wages in England,' Grandpa explained with a smile. 'In dose days cigarettes is hard to get and cigars is harder still, but I have a box of cigars bring from Miami, time before I come over here, so I carry dem in and give everybody one. Dey tek de cigar but dey look on us as interlopers, come to tek 'way dey work. Was a bad time! A fightin' time. Dey could beat you up and leave you someplace to rotten.'

'Why, Grandpa?' I asked innocently. He did not reply at once. Carefully placing a cigarette between his lips, he lit it and drew deeply and firmly as if summoning his strength from some secret place within him.

'Prejudice is for me a problem not only wid a new face but wid a dirty face. Everybody pretendin'. Everybody deep as Atlantic Ocean. Dere is a lot of talkin' but no human understandin'. To dem we is worms, creatures feedin' on rubbish dey do not want. Dey do not want de rubbish and dey do not want dem who need it to get it.'

Grandpa's lucid language never failed to give me pleasure. He had his own diction, his own imagery and words flowed from him like water. Today I wonder where those words have gone.

Before they came into this home, Grandma fell in the snow and broke her leg. At first she gave up all attempts to walk – so fearful was she of falling yet again. Grandpa talked her down the path to see the houses which were demolished behind theirs. He told her of his great love for her and led her to the place where wild flowers grew and the blackbirds sang their claim to the territory beyond. She later returned the walking frame to the hospital and reclaimed her right to walk. I am certain walking reminded her of the day, in fact the moment, when she left the Island. She was coming to join her husband but leaving her child and her parents behind.

It took time for Grandpa to establish himself and send for his wife. What did she do all those years while she waited to come to him? Was she ever unfaithful? Was he? Were there any regrets at leaving all that was hers by right, by birth and by nation? They never once talked of their loss of community love. It was as if they could think of nothing they needed that was not within them. Yet they described their early yesterdays as 'days of woe and weepin' '. Grandpa talked of those times with dread in his voice, as if reviving emotions that were bitter and burdensome. Even today they seem to understand only suffering. It is like the mortar that holds the bricks of their lives together.

'Some white people was hostileish to us,' Grandpa told me. 'Nobody offer friendship after work, Dey eyes never smile. Only dey mouth make a little move. Dey is never welcomin'. No peace within. It better if you pretend you don't notice. One time we go on a visit to Southend. I tek Auntie Gracia two girl wid us. At de beach dey never see black children, so people stop dem and tek dey photograph. When we come back we have de whole carriage to ourself. Nobody come inside to sit down near by us. Only a parson come in and den a bend-foot man – you know, handicap – and his wife. So it was we, de parson wid his dog-collar and de bend-foot man and his wife in de carriage. Dey disable by God, we disable by colour and de priest by religion.'

I laughed.

'Dey prefer to stand and block up de passage outside. You see,' he continued, 'blackness tek to count for more dan it is – skin colour. To white – some white, not all – it mean stupid, unclean,

21

low-down. No matter how you help dem or teach dem, it don't count. Dey always t'ankful but never grateful. You can never teach dem anyt'ing. Dey never admit it! Dey plead not guilty when dey do you wrong because black people never feel. Ask you grandma! Tell Tyrone about dat West End shop you sew for.'

'Chu, Simon, don't bother de boy.'

'No bother, Grandma. It's my history.'

So Grandma told me.

'I get dis job to stitch but nobody know how to cut.' She laughed at the enormity of it.

'So I cut, but another woman get de pay for de cuttin' and dey pay me as a stitcher because black can't earn more dan white in de place! Dey never invite us to a social gatherin' till de Communist Party start to collect us, and show us politics. Den de Church people shake demself and start-a-give socials for us. Dey dance wid us, hold us out at arm's length and ask where you learn English. Dey sit next to black people when dey has nowhere else to sit. You would t'ink people who give you de Bible, encourage you to watch dey mouth to learn English and teach you de alphabet and tek 'way you Africa-talk, would know dey owe you somet'ing for callin' you beast, buyin' you, sellin' you, beatin' you and sayin' you has no soul. British history bad, you know. Parson Cuthbert say dey soak de blanket wid smallpox germ and sell it to dem poor Indians in Canada. In India dey plunder, in Africa too. God know what dey done to us poor Island people!'

Grandpa never gained promotion after nearly three years in the garage, he said, and so he decided to try other ways of making money.

'To get a place to live was trouble,' he continued. 'People use to sleep anywhere – railway station, telephone booth, bus station – anywhere. To get a good work if you wasn't recruit was trouble, too. It bad to be a foreigner and worse to be coloured. But I have knowledge of abroad. I know about t'ings. Later on I start a "partner". Twenty of us pay two pound every week. It run for

22

twenty week at a time and twice a year we get forty pound each. Money in dem days. I pay down for a flat and send for Clara. Next we buy a machine and I tailor at weekend and she make dress for people in de week!'

He snatched the album and found the page which showed him sitting alone in the garage where he worked.

'I never know Carlo snap me. I ashamed of dis photo. I was de unhappiest man in de world but de foreman call me lazy. I miss my wife. I miss my son and I treated no better dan a dog. Not even a dog! Dey get good treatment! See de Queen ! Her dog get treat better dan people. Dey never slam door in de face of a dog, however scrawny. Dog have red blood like them. But dey t'ink black people have black blood, like muddy water.

'I use to go down de market on Saturday late. De market use to be full of food people throw away on Saturday. Some people use to go and pick up vegetables on a Saturday night. You never see dog dere. Dey all well fed indoors. You see people, poor Greek, poor black, poor Irish. But not a single dog. I livin' in one room sharin' a bed-shift wid another man and a toilet and bath wid as many as eat de loaves and fishes. One man sleep in de bed while I workin' daytime. When I go home at six o'clock, he go to work till seven next mornin'. So I change de bedsheet and de pillow because I have some make out of flour-bag. My mother use to buy up all de flour-bag from de baker, bleach dem and make good towels, join dem oblong by oblong to make sheet and use dem for years. Even wid clean t'ings I can't sleep because one man use to pee himself and shout out, "Don't beat me so bad, Mamma. I goin' never do it 'gain!" Den he cover his head and holler all over 'gain. De other two snore all night, one like a bull-calf and de other like a tea-kettle boilin' over. I never sleep a sound sleep till I get a place of my own and I had to try three time. Each time I pay £20 key money.'

There are pictures of Grandpa standing by the basement flat he rented. He seems pleased to have achieved something. He decorated it with help from his friends and many, with nowhere to sleep, bedded down on the floor. His sewing machine is very much in evidence.

'De boys use to order t'ings and bring de material to me. Dey prefer me to make clothes for dem because de price don't change. In de shop, soon as you ask de price it go up before you eyes. You can't argue because everybody t'ink black people stupid. You must mind you p's and q's. De police in dem long-gone days was tall, powerful men, not dem little green cucumber you meet wid nowadays! I use to feel shame when I look for a room and see "No Irish. No Blacks. No Dogs. No Children". I could never understand. Dat's why I never force Clara to bring de boy here. Children must be where dey wanted.'

I remember Grandpa's clothes, well-cut and well-pressed. Today he is smartly dressed. He is wearing a flowered tie. He had been a craftsman all his life and made clothes for men of distinction in the professions and politics. Today I feel like proclaiming him by shouting, 'Here is a man of quality and he is my grandfather!' But a little bell tinkles. Grandma and Grandpa join the surge of people making for the dining-room. I go out into the garden from where there is a clear view of the room. The old people sit at tables and are served salad which many cannot eat because their false teeth can cope with neither the coarsely chopped raw vegetables nor the leathery baked potatoes. Over-cooked prunes and custard follow. Grandpa lifts a spoonful up and smells it. He abhors the smell. He mixes everything into an untidy mess and pushes it from him. This is the signal for Grandma to feed her imaginary cat. 'Puss, puss,' she calls absent-mindedly and then dips a spoon into the mess and eats it.

There is a photograph of the cat sitting in her lap. It was called Molly. Grandma had only to stand at the door and rub two knives together to get Molly bounding out of the grass for her meal after Grandpa had eaten. Gran calls again, 'Puss, puss, puss, puss, come, come!' Her companions look at her question-ingly but say nothing. The caregivers are not around. There is no reprimand. Just the quiet acceptance of a slowly returning childhood.

24

Grandpa leaves the table and Grandma follows. I have spent one and a half hours with my grandparents.

I decide to go home but first tell the Deputy Matron that, weather permitting, I propose to take them out next time I visit.

'Where?' she asks me in an adversarial manner. I explain that they will be going to their son's house to have a proper meal – one that the old could chew and savour. She assures me that the food in the home is very good and that no one has ever complained.

I try to make some sense of this woman. In a way there is something to be said for not noticing the difference between the old and the young. She seems to ignore the fact that old people have special needs as the very youngest or the very weakest do, and that the quality of care is at the centre of the quality of the life they can enjoy. I am at a loss to decide what beliefs about life in the home she brings to her work. She is a middle-aged woman, tall and slim in build. She manages the home of around sixty old people and her work is well regarded. She sees herself however, as a kind of super woman and I am sure she thinks the same of the old men and women who have survived the rigours of their time.

I consider this woman. She does not acknowledge difference. To be different is to fail. She is feared by the staff because she is active in the union and she makes a political stew of every little thing. She is a decisive, determined woman who continuously must prove herself worthy of something known only to herself.

'By the way,' she says suddenly, 'you are getting in our way. The younger members of staff have asked a union rep to talk to you about your attitude.'

I laugh and reply nonchalantly, 'He can talk to my union rep then, can't he? I have one too, you know. Besides, I don't like how you run this place.'

I refuse to be intimidated by her union, whichever one is involved. There are no set visiting hours and, as long as I do not get in the way of the domestic staff, I feel free to come and go. Sometimes I visit between twelve and one, at other times between three and four-thirty. What harm is there in that? I write to the Matron, pointing this out, and also state that her staff constantly hassles me. I remind her that this is a 'democratic country' in which I am allowed to make a 'democratic decision' to visit my elderly relatives whom I fear are in danger of being intimidated. All this sounds like a union minute and as a consequence they stop trying to lid me in.

CHAPTER FOUR

Today it is no longer an easy matter to take my grandparents out. I can no longer say, 'Come on, Gran, Grandpa. Coat on. Hat on. We're going for a drive,' as I did after Grandpa sold his car. The caregivers refer to taking my relations out as removing them from the premises as one does the garbage. My father, of course, can take them out. He is the official next of kin. The fact that he is in poor health is of no concern to officialdom. I am the 'mouthy black'. The one who visits just to make trouble. Today I cannot find the Matron, nor the Deputy Matron, nor the Assistant Deputy Matron, although Grandma's foot is painful and I'm angry at her suffering.

'Why don't you tell someone?' I ask despairingly.

'We don't want no trouble,' they reply like a couple of parrots with a well-learned sentence. It's no use trying to convince them that 'trouble' is not the issue.

The foliage of the old oak, chestnut and other trees around the house shows the chemistry of early summer. It's a beautiful day. The blue of the sky matches a seaside postcard and buttercups like coins litter the clear, green grass. There is a kind of wary peace inside me. Suddenly there are voices in the hallway and the sound of firm, younger feet is in distinct contrast to the shuffling steps of the old folk.

The garden door opens and the visitors are well known to us. Uncle Herod is Grandpa's age but he looks at least twenty years younger. He is spry and quickwitted with none of the debilities and hindrances of old age. He is involved with his four grandchildren and could still give any young lady the business. He and Grandpa came over to England at the same time but he was

27

made of a different metal; he seized opportunity by the forelock and used it to his advantage. He brought short-lease houses, rented them at high prices to his hard-pressed countrymen and made money. He was attacked during the Notting Hill riots and fought his way from one end of his street to the other. People intent on nigger-bashing were given the corrective treatment. He had learnt kick-fighting around the Island rum shops and his attackers soon found out who was the master. The community named him 'Jujitsu' and composed a calypso in his honour. Later a young girl twenty years his junior fell madly in love with him.

When he was attacked all the humiliations he had suffered exploded inside him and, as he put it, 'It increase my strength fifty times!' Then, talking of his beautiful young wife, he added, 'I mesmerise Lurline. I had many unlawful wife but she was the first lawful one. And after thirty year no man can desire a better wife nor a better mother to children and grandchildren. She is still young to me.'

At the sight of Uncle Herod, Grandpa gives a slight start and pleasure oozes out of him, making his cheeks shine and his fingers twitch. Grandma's eyes are drawn back from their wanderings over the flowers and way beyond the fields. She smiles as Grandpa says, 'Herod! Lurline! Glad you come! Glad you come see me!'

Uncle Herod's sprightliness rubs off on Grandpa and he chatters about everything – the home, his having to retire and about the frightening eviction from his own home, his son's illness and my success at having gained admission to Cambridge. Grandma suddenly gets up and begins to totter around the garden on painful feet. Lurline reaches out for the bag streaked with dry custard on one side and other grubby bits stuck to the other. The bag in protest spills its contents – buttons, peanuts probably years old, letters, postcards, orange peel, folded-up mini plastic bags, combs of all sizes and coins in ancient cloth purses that the market women of the Island use. In the midst of everything are biscuits, chocolate and clumps of cheese.

Grandma had been a hoarder for years. I once helped my father clean their house when Grandpa was ill and she couldn't cope. The meals-on-wheels attendant brought her food and a sturdy Dominican home-help came in for three hours a week. But Grandma accused her of stealing their mahogany chiming-clock, bits of material and several other things, and threw the food at her. She refused to admit anyone after that and, when dishes of food were not taken into the house but left as an attraction for stray cats and dogs, the home-help was withdrawn. Grandma's paranoia is selective and aimed at people who come to provide any services for her.

Lurline is unsettled. She is not saying much but I can see that all her fears have been filed to razor sharpness by being here with us. I calm her by showing her the photograph of her wedding. Timidly she identifies the people in it and the talking turns towards Cousin Julinda. She is known for her ability to marry and divorce men of all ages and races. She has done it five times. She has had six children and admits to having had just enough sex for that. She is in Lurline's wedding photo, arm-in-arm with a strong-looking man. Her dress is a billowing circle of deep purple silk. I can remember one just like it hanging in Grandma's room – fashions change slowly for Island women. I hid myself in the folds of the skirt, which I pretended was an umbrella made of butterflies' wings.

Lurline offers to help Grandma with her bag. The old lady rejects her with an irrelevant remark, and Lurline is fully afraid. It shows in her face, her clenched fist and most of all in her eyes. She is afraid of old age, of becoming like this, of being treated like leftover food – frozen, discarded or, for no reason, left to decay before being thrown out. She kisses Grandma softly, in a state of sharpened, silent terror, then suddenly murmurs, 'I pray God it don't go on too long. Pray God. When I go I want to go quick. I want to go easy. That's all I want – to go easy.'

Grandma looks at her, a little surprised. But smiles and kisses her with a great sense of enjoyment.

After they are gone, we sit in silence, each a speck in time. Grandma's pride has settled in the way she holds her head. She holds it like a queen. For now she has forgotten the bag that like a ball and chain confines her to her state. Her head is majestic, like

29

a cobra's, and she holds the pose for as long as her moment of conscious pleasure lasts. Slowly her hands begin to move in circles. She is cleaning her brass jardinier again. Her mother gave it to her on her wedding day, an heirloom passed down from one generation to the next. Besides feeding the cat, it is Grandma's sole other ritual act. In this way she sheds light upon her own special darkness and keeps chaos and anxiety under control. When Grandpa was over-ambitious, all she needed to say was, 'You want us to lose everyt'ing, even my jardinier!' And Grandpa would stop himself from entering any door that was not marked 'safe' or from taking any path that was uncertain. He sometimes called her 'Cautious Clara' in fun, and caution is expressed in the way she places her heavy bag at her feet and holds the tiny bag of earth like a prayer book in her lap.

Sitting here with them makes me realise that I too am struggling to claim my place, my identity, my share. But my caution has more daring than pain. I belong, regardless of those who say I don't. Inside me there is an oasis where my identity blooms precariously and my certainties flicker like lights and then die down. This place, where my grandparents are, will destroy what is left of their bodies and even dash their spirits into the ground and they will forget just who they are and what they were in their long span of years.

Grandpa was educated in the school of life. This provided him with the words to make himself understood, and the ability to superimpose a man's figure upon uncut cloth. He could read and write enough to take him along his path. I have had to struggle to achieve because so many people expected me to do the opposite. He never once failed to encourage me. 'Tyrone,' he so often said, 'education is like an aeroplane. You can fly to heights by education.' In a way he educated himself vicariously through me. My books were his books, my homework his. I stayed with him often – a happy child in his house. My grandparents sat silently with me while I read or did my homework. Grandma often hugged me and whispered, 'Try, boy! Keep on goin'. Determi-

30

nation make hard turn easy.' I wonder what they are telling each other now.

It is time to go indoors. Grandma can hardly walk. Her foot is still swollen. I help her into the lounge. 'You had visitors, Clara,' one of the caregivers says, as if emphasising the fragility of the old woman's memory. She observes Grandma's limping. 'We have to do better than that or the doctor will have to look at our feet,' she wheedles. Grandma is sat down and given a cup of tea. It is too hot to drink. She leaves it on the table and limps off dragging her bag behind her.

'What've you got in there, Clara?' asks an old man. 'Old iron?'

'No, no, not old iron, Casey. Gold doubloons from de days of Morgan. Ever hear 'bout Morgan? He a t'ief-man but dey make him Governor of Jamaica. Poor Jamaica.'

I am astounded. Is this old woman lucid or not? Is her memory able to dart out of secret places like a spider lying in wait for prey? There is an unsuspected attack. The deed is done. The silence returns and she resumes the task of biding her time until necessity, anger or pride demands action again. Grandma and Grandpa sit side by side, hardly touching, but their lives form an indivisible link with those moments that constitute a lifetime.

I decide to ask Adijah, my girlfriend, to accompany me next time I visit. Like mine, her parents are Island people. She is petite and pretty with curling shoulder-length black hair, which she does not straighten. Her dark, almond-shaped eyes are like two brightly lit Islands in her face. Her fingers are long and slender and when she touches me she gives the impression of flowing out into life and on into my heart. Like me, she too is waiting to start her degree course but at King College, where she will study Food Science. In the meanwhile she helps her brother in his business of providing disco music for dances, parties and soirées. Their sound system is one of the best in London and they are busy with bookings for the season.

Yesterday, Grandpa always quizzed me about girlfriends and showed me the girls in the album he had fancied. He said he was timid as a young man. 'If you timid you never find gold. My brothers tek risks. Dey make money. De one name Daniel is in

31

gaol since his tricks catch up wid him. It's years since I get a letter from him.'

Grandpa knows that his brothers have died but still talks of hearing from them. He still carries old letters and postcards in his pocket. He has one I sent him when I went away with my school. I wonder what they represent in his scheme of time and things?

Grandma is asleep in her chair. The bag slips out of her hand and crashes down on the floor. She jumps awake and complains about the noise. A caregiver rushes in. 'Clara, Clara,' she snaps. 'Your bag again! It will be the death of you. Did it hurt her foot, Simon?'

'How do I know?' Grandpa says. 'I am not sittin' dere. I am here. Besides, I want my pipe.'

'What pipe, Grandpa?' I ask.

'She tek my pipe 'way.'

'You know you're not allowed to smoke in your room. You might start a fire.'

'That's fair,' I said. 'But why can't he smoke here? I'll see he returns the pipe to you for safety.'

She disappears and I am reassured. Minutes pass. Grandpa is edgy. The caregiver does not return. More minutes pass. The caregiver at last returns. She brings a pipe but it is not Grandpa's. He bursts into tears. 'I want my pipe,' he sobs. 'I buy it wid my own money. She have no right to own it. To tek it from me.' I cannot bear to see his anguish so I offer to find the pipe myself.

She motions me to silence and her eyes warn me not to interfere.

'I'll find his disgusting pipe,' she grumbles. 'I ought to know it. It's the one with the most revolting smell.'

I cover my eyes and the words which I silently hurl at her would make Satan blush.

I decide to leave.

CHAPTER FIVE

I was eighteen when my grandparents met Adijah for the first time. To Gran she represented a threat to my ambitions, an obstacle to my success. A hurricane in my life. When I passed my O-levels Gran prayed that God should lead me through my As. When I passed those with excellent grades she prayed again. This time it was that I would not become fettered by lust, wastefulness, ganja and 'disrighteousness' – while my friends rubbed them under my nose. Grandma cited examples of disrighteousness in her own family so that I could understand the meaning of the term. She talked of Julietta who was pure salt, pure pepper and pure vinegar depending on the situation.

My Gran began by being polite to Adijah, and after she had questioned her closely about her family, Gran had smiled at her. Gran would smile at a breath of air if she discovered that it came from a good family, and her smile was widest when all her curiosities had been satisfied.

Grandpa worked with enthusiasm in his garden and Adijah sometimes visited so that she could help him. I often sat with Grandma admiring the blooms, and the vegetables which attracted rabbits from the nearby fields. Sometimes hedgehogs appeared and with neat, crisp steps criss-crossed the path in search of insects. But it was Grandpa who took me to the library to seek out a book on hedgehogs when I decided to make them the subject of a short project. He was such a devoted grandfather, kind and caring and indulgent. He had missed the childhood of his only son, and relived his own more through me than my elder brother. My father came here a shy young man who had to learn to know his parents and the ways of a new country at the same time. Everything was different and that became a problem for him. He understood the simple people of his simple village. People said what they meant and did what they wanted to do. There were no grey areas, no politics in the day-to-day run of life. My father wanted to be an accountant but settled for book-keeping. The course of study was demanding and tedious after a day's work in the local laundry.

Eventually he obtained his diploma and, with all his plans altered, accepted a job on a sugar plantation back home on the Island. It had been hard to get along with his mother. To cope with her feelings of guilt at leaving her son at home for so long, she had criticised her mother through him. Nothing he did was ever right and so he had thought it better to return home. Grandpa accepted it. Grandma was bitter and hurt. How could her only son prefer her sister and her old parents to her, his mother! She had been kind to him, kept him clean, encouraged him to save his money and yet he was leaving her! It was an act of betrayal. An act against her and all that she represented, valued and believed.

Back at home, my father soon found his old self. Girls sought him out. He had been away, seen the mother country, worked and talked with white folk in an ordinary way. Perhaps he even slept with rich girls and saw their naked bodies. He fell in love with Janey Read and, as she was the most persistent, he married her in the end. She led him into politics and he became active in the Party for Democracy. He began to savour feelings of belonging to something and to someone for the first time in years. As time went on the Party for Democracy lost ground. Violence smouldered and then flared up. My father bolted to London with his family and left everything but his money behind. My brother was eight, my mother very pregnant with me. I was born soon after she arrived. There is a photograph of her and my brother picking runner-beans in Grandpa's garden. She is a mere strip of a girl and very pretty. There is a smudge of unhappiness in her eyes.

I asked Grandpa about those times. 'You mother is not patient,' he said. 'She is used to good. She want everyt'ing

34

overnight. She quarrel a lot. You father finds it hard. De constant rowing give him asthma and ulcers.'

My father worked hard and, with the help of the money he had smuggled out of the Island, bought a house at the end of a terrace. My mother grew content there. The house was small but large enough for her family and her pride. She was a capable, ambitious woman and set about earning in her own right so that she could turn her house into a home. She found employment in the linen room of the local hospital. It was boring, deadening work and she worried about leaving me with the childminder while my brother, a latch-key kid, watched television until she returned at five-thirty. Times were hard. My grandmother objected to my being left with strangers. From time to time she patrolled the street trying to get a glimpse of me and called down devils on the woman whom she was certain neglected me.

One day Grandma saw the woman busy about the market. She was sure that there was no one in the house to take care of me in particular and the other children left in the house. Entering the garden, Grandma followed the sound of screaming and found us unsupervised in the garage, all neatly harnessed in our row of prams. Grandma set off home with me but just as she opened the gate the childminder returned. 'I only left them for a minute,' she sobbed. 'I had to do the shopping. They was all asleep so I thought I would slip out for a few minutes. Please don't tell on me.' But Grandma did. My mother was shaken by the tale that was so vividly told. My father showed his pain in silence. The worry trigged his asthma. Grandma, however, got her way. She would look after us in future. I stayed with her all day and my brother made his way to her home after school. Everyone was happier. I stopped crying each morning when Mum left me and sometimes I stayed overnight with my grandparents.

I always thought of them as young. Perhaps it was because they were pure in heart and accepted that life for everyone was at that time a fierce struggle. They sought no help, asked no favours and kept to themselves. Today they sit close to sadness, close to oblivion and as delicate as seashells. It is hard to imagine them as laughing, dancing and adventurous people.

35

We went to church as a family. We were Church of England at first. 'It was a lovely church at home,' Grandma said, but when she came here she found out, clear as dew on a leaf, that the English Church did not belong to black people. 'De first time I go to church dey frighten to take communion after us, although de Parson wipe de cup. Dey watch us when we sing and ask stupid questions. That's why we join de Church of God. People pray and sing, and give God praise wid heart and voice. You tek you body to church – you use it to praise de Heavenly Father. You make a joyful noise unto de Lord.'

I too liked the Church of God. I felt a sense of release after physical, mental and spiritual participation in the act of worship. I went joyously to church with my family and sang with all my heart. Walking between my parents or between my grandparents I felt sandwiched-in and safe. I thought of myself as a boy-sandwich. I was the filling and they the slices of bread.

There is a picture of my brother Goldberg going to church. He was nineteen years old when he died. I hold the picture for a moment. Grandpa peers at it and tears slide down his crêpe-paper face and shine like oil on his cheeks. He was at our house the day Goldberg was killed.

My brother was a child of the sixties, of flower-power, love, peace and freedom. He walked dancingly down the street to some silent, intricate tunes inside his head. People noticed him and called out to him. That fatal day he went out to buy the *New Musical Express*. It was a Friday morning. He did not return. A brick was thrown at him from a speeding truck. It was a large brick. It struck him on the head. No one saw who threw the brick. They saw the dust, heard the truck, heard the brick and heard the scream. That was all. They found him on the pavement, the brick beside him, but no one could say why or how it happened. He had no enemies. He did not know how to hate.

My father took it very badly. My mother blamed her son for wearing a snow-white shirt and tight-fitting white trousers which he had made himself. 'A black boy dressed in white bound to attract hostility,' my mother said, as if it was Goldberg's fault. 'He look like a queer.' She should have hated those who killed him but she didn't even consider them. Her grief caused crooked thoughts to seep out of her and I forgave her for her callous remark. We mourned Goldberg and still do. We cremated him and left his ashes with our neighbour Mama Kane. Mama Kane kept the ashes of the dead in a special room she called the Chapel of R.I.P. There was an altar where the Holy Book, amidst ever-flickering candles and expensive artificial flowers, lay open. The urns containing the ashes of those 'waiting to go home' were neatly stacked and polished gently and tenderly. On special days visits could be arranged and, in the privacy of the chapel, visitors could speak to their dead, weep over them and relive the moment when the loved one departed this life.

Mama Kane charged nothing for this service of love. She did not believe in the scattering of ashes. 'Black people,' she says, 'were scattered in slavery. They need not be scattered in death. Bring them unto me. And I will reverently take good care of them.' Once a thief broke in to the chapel and at knife-point forced Mama Kane to open the door. She did. At the sight of the urns of ashes, all carefully labelled and polished, the thief fell down in a faint from fright, was tenderly resuscitated and then handed over to the police. Since that time thieves and house-breakers appear to bypass the house.

One day we will take Goldberg's ashes home. He never had a chance to look life in the face. He never left a mark except in our memory. Grandma often talks of him. 'When I go to heaven,' she says, 'Goldberg will help me. He will tek me round and show me de wonderful gardens of heaven. He will go to de shop and buy t'ings for me. He will help me fix my wings and we will fly and be peaceful together.'

Today I wonder if Grandma would be ready to go to heaven in spite of the burden of her bags which weigh her down. She also insists that Goldberg's death was the work of the devil, who entered the person who threw the brick.

37

The lorry was eventually traced. The driver, an old man, knew nothing about a brick. He was, he admitted, doing over thirty miles an hour in a built-up area. He was alone in his truck. Maybe someone threw the brick from the other side of the road. The police had no answers for us – only sympathy and words of consolation.

My father's health deteriorated. My mother and he grew apart but could not part and they invited the pastor to visit and pray for the return of peace and love into our home. My parents talked with the pastor about the feelings of blame and grief between them and both wept copiously. I was coming up to my secondary school and worried about what would happen if they parted. I couldn't imagine what would become of me. I became silent and sullen. The memory of Goldberg haunted me. I dreamed that he told me of his unhappiness at school and cautioned me against going to our local secondary school. I made myself ill with the fear of the future. My parents decided to pay fees and send me to a private school. I wore a uniform and worked hard. It was in keeping with the tradition of hard work in my family. I felt that I had to prove something. My heritage forbade me to stand still. I sought neither encouragement nor approval. I worked as if driven by powerful forces. I became the black boy who could. At fifteen I stood tall. At eighteen I stood taller. My family were all proud of me – my grandparents, my parents, and Adijah, my lovely girlfriend.

Looking at my photograph, I am a pleasing young man, even though I say so myself. I think I'm charming and good-looking. At school I was seen as a successful chap. Grandpa introduced me to all his friends. Sometimes he forgot and refered to me as his son. Grandma would never refer to my mother as her daughter. There has always been distance and ambivalent feelings lurking between them. Grandma knows that my father has lapses of marital loyalty and in the past helped him to cover his tracks. 'Dat's de way men is,' she sometimes said. My dad kept a change of clothes in her house for those times when he fancied a change of dish.

He must be missing this convenience now his parents have had to move.

My mum attends night school. She is determined to better herself. She is determined to get a degree and is studying for A-levels in Spanish, mathematics and English. I am able to help her. When she is at night school my father goes out on the prowl. His asthma becomes suddenly benign and I suspect helpful in his pursuit of *la dolce vita*. He enjoys sympathy which supports his fragile feelings about himself. When Grandpa talks of him he says, 'Well, de life you livin' never de life you want to live. But he is my son. I see and don't see.'

From time to time Grandma still saves a portion of cake or a dish of food for Goldberg. Then, recalling that he has gone, she mutters in a voice heavy with consternation, 'Goldberg left so sudden! It hard to t'ink dat wherever I search I never find him on de earth – in dis world.' She goes on special days to visit him at Mama Kane's. She puts flowers in the chapel and talks to his ashes. She is always subdued after a visit and reads her Bible with intense concentration. Then she says, 'You will bury me nice, Tyrone. You will, won't you, my only grandson?' And overcome with feeling, I nod and imagine the most glorious funeral in the world.

Goldberg's death puzzled me. The word 'death' held mystery for me and I felt that he had passed into another dimension of time and living that I would come to understand some day. I dreamed about Goldberg a great deal and for a long time afterwards I wore a motor-biker's helmet when I went out to the corner shop just in case a stone crashed into my head. At this point I was always at loggerheads with my mother. It was as if her heart had become one large crimson sore, the pain from which made her aggressive and even paranoid. Everything I did or said seemed to spark off fits of annoyance in her. She began to talk and gesture to herself, and the angry situations she caused ended in angrier confrontations with all of us.

I remembered the day Grandma sat her down and said gently, 'Look, girl, de people you rowin' wid stretch longer dan a clothesline. Quarrel wid one and you might be in de right. But row wid a clothesline full of people and it mean "look to youself!".' My mum did not speak. But she softened a little after that, and then suddenly she hugged me and we wept for Goldberg together.

CHAPTER SIX

Grandpa seems slightly amused today. A letter has arrived from his cousin Lucinda. 'Read it to me, Tyrone,' he says. 'You eyes younger dan mine.' I am to become very familiar with those words. I read the letter silently while Grandpa waits with patient expectation for me to come to the end of it.

'Lucinda says she is getting married, Grandpa,' I report. 'To a Mr John McBernie, a Scotsman residing in England at Her Majesty's expense. He's in prison, I mean.'

'Last time I hear of Lucinda, she in hospital in a poorly state of health,' he says in subdued surprise. 'But come to t'ink, she always in some semi-chucle* wid men, and married and t'ings such as dat.'

Grandma begins to laugh and yell. 'I hope she walkin' wid a stick. I hope she a poor old woman payin' off her debt at last.' Any talk of Lucinda brings Grandma to life. Her face darkens and she seems to be fighting her way through a jungle of years. I pass her the album. She turns the pages until she discovers a slim, pretty and open-faced woman. 'This is Lucinda,' she says. 'She follow a man name of Fraser Bine to dese shores in 1957. Is not de first married for her. Like mother, like daughter – full of love for nobody but demself. Dey like village church on Sunday – full of people, black, white and mouse colour.' Grandma is extremely lucid today.

Lucinda and her mother, Auntie Julietta, are the two most

Semi-chucle: circle.

piquant females in the family. Julietta, I have heard tell, was the village belle with an eye for the main chance. She fell in love with an Indian half-breed, too poor to indulge her expensive tastes. After a while she consented to marry Black Jack Facey, who had struck gold in one of the islands. However, she continued to meet her lover under the moon, amidst the poinsettia bushes and on the soft, yielding sand of the coconut groves.

But Black Jack Facey was promised and expected the innocence his expensive presents bought. Realising the desperate nature of her problem, Julietta turned to her two wiser and older sisters. Between them, and aided by proof-rum, ganja and certain homemade concoctions, they faked Julietta's innocence. But fate has many faces. Julietta's farewell tryst had led to pregnancy which she could not disclose before it was too late. Lucinda was born, the living image of the half-breed lover.

Jack accepted the bouncing 'seven-month' baby as his own until tongues began to wag. Jack became 'Jack the Jacket' to his friends. He proceeded to treat Julietta with punishing disregard. Amid frequent quarrels and fights he succeeded in planting a seed of his own. The result was a contrast indeed. This was Jack's child – same inky skin, flaring nostrils, heavy lips. Julietta could at last seek revenge. She made Jack's daughter Noleen, 'that high and mighty ugly man's child', a virtual slave to Lucinda. Noleen fetched and carried and carried and fetched for Lucinda who did book-work, embroidery and crochet. 'Domestic work,' Julietta said, 'would ruin Lucinda's hands.' Snow White worked for the Seven Dwarfs but Noleen slaved for an entire village. Julietta ran the village bakery and Noleen it was who worked beside her. She was separated from her sister not only by her mother-labelled 'ugliness', but by the pots, pans, bags of flour, sugar, spices, the heat of the oven and the piles of wood used to heat that oven to the right temperature for baking.

Jack denounced and then divorced Julietta, and from then on brought an army of bejewelled mistresses to his grand house. They swung their overdressed hips at Julietta and taunted her. In the end Noleen ran off to her father while Julietta ran off to the city with Lucinda.

42

Julietta soon found men, many of them, who would 'walk through fire' for her. Then it was Lucinda's turn. She too made a necklace of lovers, fat ones and thin ones, strong ones and weak ones. She too was sure they would 'walk through fire and swim rough water' for her. She got many babies and washed away all save one.

'My men respect me and my body too much!' she boasted. I sleep with them for company. None would dare touch my shoulder, night, morning nor middle-day, and say, 'Lucinda, "roll-over".' She was a pathetic woman with only the songs of her specious life to sing. All this my mother would disclose whenever my father upset her.

'You know, Tyrone,' Grandma says out of the blue. 'Julietta de treble voice and Lucinda de alto. Nothing will come of dis weddin'. It will puff away like silk cotton seed.' She totters into the lounge in an angry state of mind. But as she says nothing more it is difficult to tell how she really feels about the wedding.

'Go see Lucinda, Tyrone,' says Grandpa. 'Find out de facts of de matter.'

But I do not have to go at all. The next week I visit early because every Tuesday the librarian calls with a trolley of ancient books. It really amuses me to see the way these old men and women stick to the writers of their youth. As I stand and watch the librarian trying to influence their choices, a taxi draws up and a little old woman carefully climbs out. She enters the lounge, her eyes darting about like a spotlight, and follows me as I walk to the garden where my grandpa sits. She does not seem to recognise my grandpa straight away, but as he sits stiffly on the seat something about his overall features must have reminded her. 'Simon?' she asks in a voice that shows she is strong enough to queue up for her pension and walk to the polling station to vote against anyone she feels would be unsupportive of her beliefs. 'Young Simon Grainger!' she says.

Gandpa looks at her and his eyes soften. 'Julietta,' he says, 'my own, sweet cousin. Glad you come see me. I get you letter. Meet me grandson Tyrone. He swallow down books one after de other. He goin' to Cambridge next year. I hear 'bout de weddin'.'

Sitting down, Julietta gives me a sideways look. She doesn't like my dreadlocks.

'Well, Simon, God is a mysterious God. I want to see Lucinda fix up permanent before I go home to heaven and God answer a widow-mother prayer. I getting on, you know! And I drop Lucinda when I eighteen!' She laughs nervously. Grandpa pulls out his pipe, lights it and blows his thoughts away with the smoke.

'Where Lucinda meet her intended?' he asks contemplatively.

'Oh, in the hospital, you know. Now a day they mix everybody up. No man ward. No woman ward. Lucinda go into hospital because her kneecap troubling her. She sit in the common room, sad and alone, and this nice man come by her and kiss her hand ready to 'walk through fire for her'. It was her luck come straight to her and touch her. Lucinda, big as she is, act like a child sometimes.'

'Which country he come out of? Africa?'

'God, no. Africa. Thank God not one of them. I can't stand them. Too savage. Out of Scotland.' Then lowering her voice she adds, 'He go to prison – years ago now, for choking his wife to nearly dead in a row 'bout money.'

'Eh! Eh!' says Grandpa. 'And you give you consent? Murder in de family? Julietta, "nearly dead" from you mean dead. Dat's dangerous matters. Dead is dead. You prefer him to a good, clean, godfearin' African like Bishop Tutu? Nobel Prize?'

'Well, Simon. She go in the hospital for sickness and come out with love. And I can's say no more. He nearly done his sentence and he and Lucinda turn to God. They flowering in love like them rice in the cornfield.'

Grandpa gives a heavy sigh but I can see he is still conversing with his doubts. I know what she means even if she doesn't. Rice in the cornfield, indeed! One needed water and the other didn't.

'I'll take Gran and Grandpa to the wedding when the time comes – let us know,' I say, intruding upon the embarrassment that hovers between them like a bird.

'I better not see your wife, Simon,' Julietta says abruptly, ignoring my offer. 'She don't like me and I don't like her ever

44

since we was little. I see sun five years before her and yet she never respect me – I never forget how she take over my granddaughter Mydral.'

Anger is thickening inside Julietta like cornflour on the boil, but her taxi is still waiting and she leaves. Grandpa opens the album and shows me a plump young girl with a strong, intelligent face carrying a basket of flowers.

'Dat is Myrdal,' he says. 'She got a child in our kitchen. It nearly strike us dead dere on de spot.'

I knew the story well. My mother's rages never allow her to omit this tale which she describes as 'shocking enough to draw a cold from the devil's chest'.

Myrdal found school a chore and took to truanting. She was liberal in her dealings with the young lads she met during her wanderings. She lied her way out of one kind of trouble and ended up in others of a more telling kind. She became a gymslip mother at fifteen, and much too young for maternity classes. She feared an abortion more than the police and, dreading encounters with both her mother Lucinda and her grandmother Julietta, she ran away from home and hid herself at Grandma's house. From then on she had no contact with either of them. Grandma welcomed her, ignored the fact that she was so pleasantly plump and gave her the love she craved. And then early one morning they heard a kind of mewing in the kitchen. Out of sheer curiosity Grandpa wandered in and found Myrdal and her beautiful baby. 'I never know you do dig-jig,' Grandpa said, bewildered. 'I thought you was a miss and now you is a mistress.'

In hospital the baby was tended and adored for its form and perfection even though its mother was so young. Myrdal named him Simon and gave him up for adoption to a white couple. Years later he came looking for his mother and no one could help him. But at the time of his birth she did not know how she came by him. 'I can't remember the right man,' she had said. 'Someone made me drunk with vodka.'

'Was it a black man give you vodka?' Grandma probed. 'Rum is black man drink. I know it for true.'

'It must have been a white man because I know it was vodka I drink.'

'We is family, Simon,' Grandma pleaded. 'What can we do but help poor Myrdal? She is not responsible for her condition.'

'She is!' Grandpa affirmed. 'She is! She not a yard-hen looking for a cock. Drinking vodka is going to Russia. Is bad.'

When news of the birth reached Julietta, she was furious that the baby had been adopted. The row with Grandma is legend. Words were used like knives and they made permanent cuts on Grandma's heart. Lucinda, a dab hand with switch, stick or strap, gave Myrdal the beating of her life. Then she locked the young mother in a cupboard with a cup for her tears, and fed her bread and water for a week. Myrdal managed to escape and took a train to where no one could ever find her. No one did. And to this day no one knows whether she is dead or alive. Grandma believes she eventually married and went to live in Africa. Africa is a huge continent and Lucinda wrote her off referring to her as 'my dead daughter Myrdal that shame me and let me down'.

There are pictures in the album of Gran and Julietta with a group of women enjoying a picnic. Gran is not as beautiful as Julietta, but her lovely white dress, seductively fitted at the waist, flows out to show the joyousness of the occasion. Today her eyes are watery and her face crinkled and surrendered to time. Grandpa is also at the picnic, smart in white trousers, blazer and boater. 'I was young when I was young,' he says. 'In every way a true and perfect man.' Ignoring him, my Gran scratches her head.

'Tyrone,' he says, from some faraway spot in her mind. 'My mama come see me today or I dream? I sure somebody come and bring me cornbread but it ent nice like my make.'

'Julietta came to visit but she came empty-handed. She didn't bring cornbread,' I explain.

I can remember the cornbread my gran used to make. It was light and melted in the mouth, like food for the blessed. My brother and I used to fight over the last piece.

'I'll ask Adijah to make cornbread for you, Gran.' I remark. But her attention has moved from her cornbread to her foot.

'My foot hurtin', I can't walk to meet wid him. My father I mean. I want him come tell me about dese doubloons he give me. Doubloons is pirate money? Some good and some bad?'

Grandpa, a troubled look on his face, hugs her – or tries to hug her.

'Simon,' she says sharply. 'An old man like you huggin' people up? You too spoil. Is you mother fault. She spoil you. I never spoil my son.' Like children, their moods shift and change with almost confusing suddenness.

Grandpa laughs heartily. His pipe has been returned and his pride retrieved. I am happy that I could have done for him today what he did for me, so long ago when I was twelve years old and wore short trousers and a school blazer.

Each day as I walked home I was stopped by a young policeman, Constable Keeler – who years later, promoted to sergeant, was to officiate at my grandparents' eviction. He picked me out of the group and ostentatiously searched me on the pavement.

'I haven't done anything,' I'd protest. 'Cut me and I bleed.' I had heard that on the TV and was bursting to say it out loud.

'No lip out of you, sunshine.' His voice, though soft and jokey, was dripping threat. His smile was menacing, yet friendly. I was confused. Who was this man? A friend? An enemy?

'I'll tell my father,' I sob. 'You stop me every day. You pick on me. Why?'

'Don't you know why, sunshine? I'm only doing my job.'

I felt vulnerable and powerless and hurried home. I burst into the room and told my father. Anger had tripped my throat and I could hardly talk. He turned on me.

'What you fussing for? They search me as well. Not a day pass. They look for drugs. They're trash with power.'

The searching continued and I wilted before my peers. My difference was a disease, and when the policeman taunted, 'OK, sunshine' – or ram, or cock – 'see you tomorrow,' I died in my twelve-year-old boots. What did my father mean? What was 'trash with power'?

'I am not sunshine,' I protested. 'My name is Tyrone Grainger.'

'You don't mean it, Mr Lippy! Now where did you get a nice British name like that!' he asked derisively.

I began to refuse school. Getting up in the morning was more than an effort. I tried desperately to make myself sick. Grandpa took matters in hand and telephoned a representative of the West Indian Standing Conference. Together they visited the police station with me.

'My grandson is not a villain,' my grandpa said. 'He is a decent child from a decent home. No ganja dere. No dope dere. Do unto others.'

The policeman never stopped me again. I loved my grandpa so much my heart felt light and happy again. We sat down to a large slice of cake each. and talked as we did before I was hounded by fear of policemen. I remember the taste of that slice of cake to this day. It took all my anxieties away. On the morning of the eviction, the police held no terrors for me, or indeed for any of us.

Grandpa said, 'You know, Tyrone, white people don't understand black people is people too. I meet it first time back home. I have a uncle name of Cyril and he is gardener for some white people name of Tyson. All de little shirt-tail white children, three or four year years old, used to call him Cyril. One day I ask him why dey don't call him Uncle Cyril or Brother Cyril or Mr Cyril like little boys and girls in de yard. He say, "Simon, dey is white and we is black and dey believe dey better. But when dey dead dey stink just like any other man." After dat I never 'fraid for white – barrin' my Uncle Dandeau false teeth. Dey was lily-white, even when dey float about in his mouth. Not only black t'ings can frighten people.'

In spite of all Grandpa said, I was still terrified, distrustful and fearful of whites. My encounter with the police left me feeling disembodied and anxious and marked me for years. I could not understand a conception of hatred that was directed to certain people, and permanently fixed upon them. My grandparents hated no one and were not changed by their encounters with racism. But to me, Grandma's burdensome bag showed the powerlessness that comes to the poor and the oppressed people in the world. As I grew older I became more conscious of the need to defend my ground and fight my corner. To me aggression, anger and hate were normal responses to persecution and racial attack.

Grandma is sitting still today. Her inner thoughts are oozing out of her in a harsh scraping voice. She is singing as she sang long ago when she was happy or troubled, or winning at dominoes or some other game:

> 'O, we need love's tender lessons taught,
> As only weakness can.
> God hath his small interpreters
> De child must teach de man.'

'Shut up, Clara,' the old woman beside her shouts. 'You people are too noisy!' But Grandma scrapes away. There is a light in her eyes. She begins to clean her brass jardinier again, and continues to sing in full flood.

> 'De haughty eye shall seek in vain,
> What innocence beholds.
> No cunnin' finds de key of heaven
> No strength its gate unfolds.'

'Shut up, you bitch!' the woman yells again. Grandma still sings on but changes tempo and tune.

> 'Angry words! Oh, let dem never
> From de tongue unbridled slip.
> May de heart's blest impulse
> Check dem, ere dey soil de lip.
> Love one another! Thus said de saviour . . .'

The trolley rumbles by. Tea is about to be administered. Grandma puts down her bag and sits up like a cat anticipating a woollen ball.

49

'Hello, Clara!' the caregiver says. 'You'll have a drink today? I know you love coffee. I've made you a cup special.'

Grandma breaks out in a new frenzy of song. With eyes half closed, she is conducting the melody.

> 'A fitly spoken word
> It hath mysterious powers;
> Its far-off echoes shall be heard
> Ringing through future hours.
> An hones', truthful word
> It has a tongue of flame
> On wings of wind it flies abroad
> And wins a heavenly fame.
> Speak, for de love of God!
> Speak for . . .'

'Gran,' I interrupt. 'Look, your favourite sweet. Butterscotch!' She gives me a lovely smile, accepts it and pops it into her mouth. It is the only way to stop her singing.

'I'm going, Gran,' I say. 'Goodbye.'

'Where you goin', Tyrone?' she asks sadly.

'To the West End, Gran. We're picketing a store that is still selling golliwogs.'

'Don't do dat, Tyrone!' Grandpa chips in. 'Long ago people try to do dat. It make no difference. Dey believe blacks *is* golliwog. Don't waste time! Ask Herod. When he young he picket 'gainst the minstrel show, but all he get is a brick in his face.'

'I know, Grandpa,' I say determinedly. 'But we mustn't give up.'

Grandpa bites into his pipe and Grandma waves – a little wave – tiny in the expanse of time without change.

CHAPTER SEVEN

Something unusual must have happened. I am summoned to the Matron's office. It's a bright, airy, well-appointed little room with long canary-coloured curtains smudged with patterns of brown. The two armchairs are upholstered in a lighter shade of brown and the wall-to-wall carpet is a deep, clear gold. It is altogether a pleasant room and I make myself comfortable while I await the entry of this astringent woman. She enters the room like a wind rushing to disturb the peace of sitting down in a clean and tidy room.

'What have I done now?' I ask resignedly.

'Nothing, Mr Grainger! Don't be so thin-skinned, so touchy. I'm vexed with your gran, really vexed with her. She poured a whole jug of water over her head and wet-up everything.' The Matrons' diction and pronunciation do betray some West Indian contact.

That struck me when I visited the Islands on a school tour. The white creoles spoke in the same twang, ate the same kind of food and behaved in the same way as the black creoles. Perhaps the Matron is a creole who has come home.

'Did she? I say. 'Maybe she wanted a bath. She hates being left in the bath for hours while the caregivers watch serials, funnies and films on the telly. It's a fact. Ask Belladora.'

She ignores my remark and then says, 'Your gran wants her hair washed. We tell her she has to wait.'

The need to defend Gran flares up inside me like a struck match. 'Why must she wait? She isn't a naughty child. They're all old in here. Some get, but some must wait.'

'Mr Grainger, you must know why! We are not used to her sort of hair. It takes effort and understanding. We can't exactly put a comb through it, now can we?'

'Hair is hair,' I retort crisply. 'Dab some shampoo on it, pour water over that, stir the lot with your fingers and the hair will wash. My grandmother has rights and one is to be kept clean.'

'I know, I know, Mr Grainger, and her rights are our responsibility. Why do you tear-up yourself? Always wearing a hair-shirt trimmed with politics?'

She has pulled the wrong switch and smiles apologetically when she realises what she has done.

'I'll ask my mum to come over. It won't take her ten minutes to wash my grandma's hair.' The intonation in my voice is fierce.

'All I'm saying, Mr Grainger, is that we need someone patient and competent to wash your gran's hair.'

'You're making out that my gran is a problem. You should have had a competent nurse to see to her foot straight away, not waited while it got worse. It's always difficult for you if it's anything to do with our people.'

'That has given me an idea,' she says, softening. 'I'll ask the same nurse to do it since you mentioned her.'

I backtrack. 'I should not have got angry. Understanding the old is your work. They are just old children who disobey. You see, we're going to a family wedding. And my gran worries about herself.'

'A wedding!' she exclaims. 'I had a wedding day. And that's not a wedding, especially during the war.'

'You look much too young to have seen the war,' I say.

She laughs, sits upright in the chair and looks into the mirror on the opposite wall.

'Mr Grainger,' she says. 'Don't think we're against your people. We're not.' She gives me one of her sweet, scheme-concocting smiles. It seems to go on for minutes. I smile back briefly and hurry out to my grandparents.

They are nowhere to be found, but as I scurry down the corridor I hear the sound of an untuned piano being played with great verve. Voices, some cracked, some surprisingly melodious, are singing in accompaniment to several well-known old music hall tunes. At the piano sits a man I have never seen before. He is obviously a new admission. He has a full white beard but his sharp nose gives a distinctive silhouette to his features. He is wearing a light grey tweed jacket and terylene trousers and obviously enjoying the way he affects the other inmates. They come tottering out of their rooms with walking sticks or walking frames.

'Is it Christmas?' asks an old woman in a bright, agitated voice. 'Why are you having fun?'

The singing lasts till close on lunchtime, and when the choir has shuffled in for their meal I talk to the old man. He is lightly built, spry, about five feet ten in height. He is well educated, and old in years alone. He is nearly ninety, has survived his entire family, two world wars, unemployment in the thirties and whatever else life has cared to throw at him. His life story pours out of him like water from a tap turned on.

'I'm George,' he tells me eventually.

'I'm Tyrone Grainger, sir,' I reply.

'I guess those are your old folk. My mother, bless her, let lodgings to a Negro sailor when I was a boy. They were always here, the Negroes. Only there's more now. You know Queen Elizabeth, the Virgin Queen, asked them all to leave once?'

I nod.

'Our lodger, he was a peculiar chap. I can't recall where he came from but he used to lay out his money carefully. "Dis for my belly. Dis for my back." ' He laughs at the memory. 'Had his dinner with us once a year. When we moved to Goldington, he went. I never saw him again. Nice man. He used to give me a penny each week. He was very respectful to Mother. Bless her soul. She was a wonderful woman. Father died and left her with five children, four boys and a girl, to bring up. It was a real struggle for her but she did it. No criminals amongst us, and we fought for King and country.'

'Well, if the other four were like you, your mother must have been a proud woman.'

'I'm the only one left. I've put them all down. I was the weak one. Never expected to live. I had brain fever at eight and

53

tuberculosis of the hip at thirteen. Yet in the Great War I was in the King's Royal Rifles and one of the scouts in a battalion of a thousand men.'

I interrupt his reminiscences to ask, 'Aren't you hungry?'

'No, no, I don't eat much. And what I've seen of the meals in here, they're barely appetising. Besides, I had porridge for breakfast with salt. The way the Scots do.'

'Are you from Scotland?'

'No, I'm English. My father was a German-speaking Huguenot. He came here when the French were after them. We spoke German at home and I used to go to German school every Saturday. They taught us music too. I used to pay sixpence a week. I was born round St Pancras. The Huguenots were great craftsmen. There were a lot of churches round there and they used to do all that sort of work – the carvings and that. My father was a cabinet-maker at Maples till he died. All his brothers were craftsmen.'

'Are you sure you're not hungry?'

'No, really. I have to eat little and often. My stomach went kaput some years ago. Perforated!'

A caregiver brings him a cup of tea and he sits sipping it, his bright eyes burning holes into his yesterdays. I linger, fascinated now by his talk about his life in the trenches and the death of his friend.

'So sudden it was. One minute he was talking, the next he was gone. The Huns put a shot between his eyes. A neat little hole. A trickle of blood. That was all. That shot took away my faith. I used to believe if I kept myself pure, God would preserve me. I did but my arm was nearly chopped off with shrapnel. My mother received a letter saying I had died. But I was still after the Huns. One day they were just ahead of us. We came on a store of their bread – hundreds and hundreds of loaves of bread each one sour, each one like a lump of the hardest rock. We were so hungry we ate some. I went on ahead. That's where I got wounded. They missed me by a hair's breadth. For months I was in a hospital in France. I could not put my hand on my head. But

54

after I was discharged and sent home, Mother worked on me and soon I was good as new.'

The drops of tea on his beard, like rainwater on grass, seep through to his chin and I go off to get him a handkerchief. He will not use tissues.

When I return he is singing softly to himself. The song, he says, tells of the love of a French soldier for a German nurse. He sings the words line by line in the language of each lover, one line in French, the other in German, the melody tumbling out of his mouth like kittens at gentle play. Suddenly he stops and goes back to the piano, runs his fingers along the keyboard in some of the most mystifying arpeggios I have ever heard and then breaks into 'Won't You Come Home, Bill Bailey?'

Belladora leaves the table. Her friends, laying down their cutlery, clap. Leaning on her walking stick, she manages to sit down close and then in deep melodious tones gives us the whole syncopated story

'On one summer's day, sun was shining fine,
The lady love of old Bill Bailey was hanging clothes on de
  line
In her back yard, and weeping hard.
She married a B and O brakeman,
Dat took and throw'd her down.
Bellering like a prune-fed calf, wid a big gang hanging
  round,
And to dat crowd she yelled out loud:
"Won't you come home, Bill Bailey, won't you come
  home?"
She moans de whole day long;
"I'll do de cooking, darling, I'll pay de rent,
I knows I've done you wrong.
'Member dat rainy eve dat I drove you out
Wid nothing but a fine tooth comb.
I know I'se to blame, well, ain't dat a shame?
Bill Bailey, won't you please come home?"'

I throw my arms around her. 'Man,' I say, 'you're good! Better than Cleo Laine, the Queen of Jazz.'

She pushes my hands away.

'Young man, I hate jazz. But that was all I could sing,' she says icily. 'They forced me into blackness. I wanted to be a person. First they made me an issue. Then they made me a problem.' She limps away, sits in her chair and, closing her eyes, she too walks the labyrinth of her yesterday.

'Belle can be extremely rude,' says a caregiver. 'The Matron is the only person she sees as her equal in here. Ignore her behaviour. She is often in great pain. She was an entertainer but all she wanted to sing was coloratura arias. Her father was an African sailor and her mother an English girl from Liverpool. She experienced a great deal of racial prejudice. At school, at work. In life.'

Grandma comes towards me. 'All dat singin' and nice music full my cup of happiness to overflow. George tickle dem ivories like if God bless his hands. A righteous man, George is.'

She loves music. Her sister, she's always said, was the organist at their church and she knows a great many religious chants and hymns. Words are falling out of my grandmother like coconuts from a basket at a village market. She is once more seeking friendships and contacting others.

'How you learn to play piano so good?' she asks George.

'I used to go to music lessons. A German woman in Alþany Street. It cost sixpence a week. My father was a cabinet-maker but I was sickly so I followed my own trade. I was a barber. I hated it so to get out of it I became a soldier. In the army I played in the mess and after the war I had time to play every day – I was unemployed for years. Now if you want a bob or a Greta Garbo cut, Clara, just knock on my door!'

'You can cut Simon hair,' she replies. 'Opportunity is a wonderful t'ing,' she adds as if in a reverie. 'If you have opportunity you can be clever like George. If you was poor and black, opportunity for you would be holdin' on to a bag of thorns. I glad you have brain, Tyrone. Head make to hold brains. Not to wear hat.'

George often sits with us in the garden. From time to time he trims what's left of Grandpa's hair, and pleads with me to let him cut off my dreadlocks. He tells us stories of well-dressed men of the past, of Beau Brummell and Champagne Charlie. Of great music-hall figures like Nosmo King who, it was said, took his name from the 'no smoking' sign in the underground train that took him to work at a West End theatre. And George tells us of the Second World War and his job as a stretcher bearer. 'I saw much sadness, much anguish, much suffering. I never once saw God,' he says.

Grandma tells him of the forthcoming wedding. Patting her arm, he says, 'If my sister was still walking this earth, she would have done a Madame Pompadour for you. She was a hairdresser and wig-maker to a man named Nestler. He singed off all his wife's hair trying to invent a perm for women. Then he started practising on my sister's hair. He permed it and some other chap – can't remember his name after all these years – claimed the invention. They went to court and Nestler won the case and kept his patent. My sister gave evidence. You can read it yourself in the Public Records Office if you have a mind to. She had her hair permed before anyone else ever did!'

My grandparents are becoming more coherent with the passing of each day. They have stopped deteriorating. I can hardly believe the evidence of my eyes. Grandma has moved from spasms to spans of clarity. She is becoming a part of things. She forgets her burden-bag from time to time, and sits in the garden among the birds and flowers, and notices the clouds. It is an almost miraculous change and I feel grateful for it.

I go home now full of happiness that her foot is on the mend. We have not abandoned the old people after all! The bits of understanding, enjoyment and self-awareness that have been falling off them now all stay in place. They are living, thinking people again.

My father's asthma appears to be under control and he too is looking forward to meeting his relations at Lucinda's wedding.

My mother, however, is none too keen. To her Lucinda is pretentious, opinionated and selfish. 'For an old woman she should learn to show gratitude instead of thinking that whatever you do for her, you supposed to do. I am not going to any wedding. I am not spending out on that ungrateful old bag. No present from me!'

Adijah, who has just arrived, begins to laugh. Dad makes a face behind my mother's back and whispers, 'My wife seems grudgeful of a beautiful woman.'

'Who grudgeful? When last you see that old bag? Neck like a tree root and the lines on her face like wire netting. Handsome girl with dirty tricks. That's Lucinda.'

My mother is in good form! Later it's agreed that on the day of the wedding I will fetch Grandpa and Gran from The Birches, pick up Uncle Herod and take them all to the venue in my car. Mum, who decides to attend after all, will drive Adijah, Lurline and Dad in hers.

The next day is warm and fresh and everything goes according to plan. Grandma, slippered on her bad foot and shod on her good, volunteers to leave her bag behind and sits expectantly in the car with Grandpa. After we pick up Uncle Herod they start giving each other riddles as we go. They are some of the most ancient riddles I've ever heard. It is a ridiculous way of passing the time and I cringe when they yell 'Give up' and giggle like three- or four-year-olds. After a very short while I become so bored with their childish talk that I regret my choice of company.

Mercifully the prison comes into view. I turn sharply and drive along a smooth, hedge-lined road until we reach the entrance to a century-old, monolithic structure with the appearance of rigour and 'heavy manners' about it. It seems angry at the deeds of men. Only the backdrop of clouds piled high in the clear blue of the sky softens the outline of this soulless place. I cannot decide whether it has been robbed of its homeliness because it is a prison or whether it is a prison because of this lack.

'We're here, Gran,' I say. 'Let me help you out.'

She refuses my help and pushes her head out of the open door. 'Dis is a funny church,' she murmurs. Then, raising her voice, she asks, 'Why dis church don't have a cross on top? Church should have cross on top like St Paul Cathedral, the Queen Church, and like St James-the-Less back home. I christen in dat church, I married in dat church and I ent goin' in dis one. I ent eatin' hard cornbread in my evenin' life.'

She straps herself back into her seat carefully and competently and says, 'I want go back where I come from.' She has completely forgotten why she has dressed up and why she has come all this way.

Nothing can persuade her to get out of the car. I wonder if this is the echo of her encounter with the racist mob several months before. In the meantime the others have also reoccupied their seats.

'Grandma,' I explain. 'This is not a church. It is a gaol. Lucinda is marrying someone in prison. They've changed the law like they did in America. Last week a woman married a prisoner. It was in the papers. This week cousin Lucinda is doing it.'

Gran becomes greatly agitated. 'My mother never make one of us to be gaolbird. Oh my God, save a poor sinner from de clutches of Satan!' she wails.

Uncle Herod hugs her as the other car arrives.

'You go in!' I exclaim. 'We're going back to The Birches. Gran is upset by the prison. She feels unhappy and suspicious.'

All the while Grandpa says nothing. He leaves me to cope with the difficulties and keeps up his conversation with Herod. On the way home Gran rants on about Julietta and Lucinda. 'One made you eye-water run, de other made you teeth edge. One was de snake, de other de grass.'

'Gran, stop it!' I say sharply. 'You're too old to quarrel.'

Darting a look at me, she lets the remark she would have made die on her lips. Resonating anger makes me struggle to control myself. It would do me no good to be involved in an accident on Lucinda's wedding day, however I feel about it.

The roads are crowded and we take much longer to return. I feel really upset at myself for letting my grandparents waste my time. I have taken a year off. I could have gone abroad like so

59

many of my contemporaries. Gone to distant parts of the world –
chancing my arm, and chasing my luck. Instead here I am,
young and strong, dancing attendance on two recalcitrant,
ageing children, being their parent and indulging them. I am so
frustrated at my own stupidity I feel like weeping. But men
shouldn't weep, should they? And so I convert my feelings into a
grotesque smile and carry on.

CHAPTER EIGHT

I call at our home on the way back and we all have some refreshments before returning to The Birches. Who could have foreseen Grandma's reaction? Eventually she calms down, drinks her tea and is happy to be back on her seat in the garden. Uncle Herod and I amble down to the end of the garden and watch the sparrows arguing and fighting over large slices of stale bread.

'It's funny of Lucinda,' he muses. 'She like she got a conjure on her! Man after man, marriage choked dead time and again. This man love me! Oh, he so love me! This man will give his eyeball for me! And what come of it? Nothing. She living in a pensioner flat the Council give her. What she got to show for life? Hats, shoes, plenty clothes and a chile who never reach for her. I think she might have two but I sure 'bout one.'

Grandpa sits talking to George. It is his turn today to hear the old Englishman's stories again.

After a while I leave The Birches. I am consumed with the desire to meet Adijah and hear about the wedding and so hurry home. I am still in a smouldering rage. If my parents say one wrong word I will explode like a banger on Guy Fawkes Night. When Adijah finally comes in with my parents she appears to have had a really enjoyable time.

'It was OK,' she says. 'You couldn't tell the prisoners from the guests. The best man forgot the ring, though, and Julietta had to pull one of hers off so the wedding could go on.'

'What's the bridegroom like?'

'Stocky, pale, puzzled and intense. He seemed eager to marry her. She's older, I should say. The Governor and some other

61

officials were there. They even had a priest. It was a real wedding. Honest!'

'Did Mum enjoy meeting her family – or rather, Dad's?'

'Your mother just watched. She said little. She avoided talking to Lucinda. They all said how nice your mother looked.' Then she added, 'Lucinda received a condolence card this morning.' Someone felt so sorry for her that they sent her deepest sympathy. She looked at your mum when she wondered who had sent it!'

'They always blame my mum. For everything,' I say. 'My mum says they envy her for her life with my dad. My mum and dad are friends, really. All the others are either strung-up or divorced. He has strayed but it's been of no consequence, he's stayed.'

Adijah laughs so prettily I imagined that fragrant flowers encircle her. She is so full of fun and good sense, I am happy that she is my friend. She belongs to life and I am allowed to walk beside her. I tell her about Gran – how she has stretched my patience to the limit – and how I feel about going back to see both of them again. 'I love my grandparents but visiting them as often as I do is becoming a burden,' I say. 'I took the year off so that I could help my dad, but recently it has become a chore. I can't cope with the moods and the swings.'

She comes and stands beside me and then hugs me reassuringly. I feel safe in her love and my doubts ebb away. 'Childhood comes first,' I say. 'And then it comes after.'

'It keeps on coming after,' she laughs.

For two days I do not visit The Birches. I miss George's music, his stories and his laughter but it will help if my gran in particular misses me a little. When I return on the Wednesday the old folk are sitting around the television set but ignoring the cricket commentary. From time to time the pitter-patter of cheers that mark a classic stroke startle those closer to consciousness. The others doze on, bobbing like boats on the seas of past and present. The clinking of the ubiquitous tea-trolley elicits a blink or two from some of them and then all is quiet again. Silence, like the tentacles of some invisible creature, slowly enfolds them all, dissolves them and then absorbs them. But the silence is neither alive nor creative. It is the silence of resignation, disquietude and impending oblivion.

A caregiver greets me with a smile. 'Mr Grainger, your old people missed you,' she says. 'They're not a bit of trouble but they get restless if you don't come.'

'Where are they?' I ask, adding, 'That's a turn up for the book! You no longer mind if I visit?'

'It's a bit colder but they are in the garden. A young woman is with them,' she replies ignoring my query.

Happily Adijah is with them, and they are talking about the wedding. I suggest that we move to the bar. It is a long room with a window at one end, and from this drinks can be bought for two hours each day. Grandpa is certain that all the drinks are watered – gin, brandy or whisky. He shouts out his conviction while playing snakes and ladders and Chinese chequers. Grandma, I feel, knows that she has upset me, and keeps off the subject of Lucinda's wedding in my presence. She talks instead of village sport, and the pleasures of it. In her salad days Grandma was the captain of the village rounders team and the champion chequers player. The moves begin to surface as she plays game after game, and she twitters like a bird and deftly carries her chequer marbles forward.

Suddenly there is life in the lounge below us. The piano is wide-awake again. George has returned. He plays for some forty minutes before joining us for a drink. He is smartly dressed in a dark grey wool suit, white shirt and pale blue tie. As he proceeds up the stairs, Belladora calls out, 'It won't be long, George, before you'll be given cast-offs like us. Clothes disappear in here.' Fortunately she is not overheard.

As usual George talks of his mother. 'When that lovely woman forsook this world of woe, my brother that ran off and got married wrote to us after the funeral to ask for his share. We wrote back saying that apart from the funeral expenses there was nothing to share. We never heard from him again. It wasn't him, you know. It was his greedy, beady-eyed, grasping wife that he gave up his widowed mother and a good home for.'

He pauses and lights his pipe.

'You know, Mother wore black from the day Father died to the day she died at ninety-nine and a quarter. She was a widow for over sixty years. Always in mourning, like Queen Victoria. When I was a boy, I used to see Victoria the Good riding in her carriage!'

Apart from the Great War and the Second World War, love for his mother is his most absorbing topic of conversation. His voice changes tone, his eyes soften and his manner becomes reverential.

'Well,' I say, 'your mother is in heaven now with God.'

'Yes,' says Grandma. 'In due course we all go home.'

'Where is your bag, Grandma?' I ask, surprised to see her empty-handed.

'I put it up. I put it up. Take it home, Tyrone. I get it for you.'

'Did you say God, Tyrone?' George asks in controlled astonishment.

I nod.

'You know, Tyrone, if God made this world and allowed people to do some of the things they do, I don't think much of Him. When people are crippled, shot in the head, blown to bits. Is that God? I loved my brother Arthur. He died in mortal pain. They have all gone. Is that God? No, Tyrone, heaven is here, hell is here, and we are here.'

I ignore his outburst, and gesture at a box beside him. 'What's in there?'

'It's a tape recorder and some tapes of classical music. I heard all the great tenors and sopranos of the past and prefer this kind of music. My great-nephew plays an electric guitar. I never heard such a racket in my life.'

He talks to Adijah about the wedding at the prison and is surprised that such a thing could be allowed to happen. 'When a man goes to prison, he should be punished. A man goes to prison to reform,' he says. 'I suppose they drank champagne at the ratepayers' expense.'

'No, we took our own,' says Adijah.

'Well,' says George. 'People search for what makes them feel at ease with themselves wherever they are.' He hurries to his room.

64

He has a sense of morality I can't quite fathom – liberal about some things and reactionary and conservative about others.

Outside autumn is approaching. The leaves are changing colour. Pointing out the strong rush of browns and greens, Grandma seems concerned that someone has set fire to the spreading chestnuts and oaks in the park.

'The park set on fire,' she shouts. 'People wicked, wicked. When t'ings bad at home and people want work, dey sneak in de fields to burn de cane, bring up de sap and chase out snakes and other evil. Look it, over there!'

It's autumn, Grandma – then winter will come.'

She nods, thinks and aborts her reply.

'My foot better today,' she says suddenly. 'But Grandpa lost his pension money and his letters. He upset his mind.'

Without another word I head to the laundry, rummage around and retrieve two tacky yet important strands of his identity. I am angry with him but try not to show it. How many times have I told him not to leave those papers in his pocket? When he gets them back, he is so happy I cannot bear to reprimand him. He opens the album and points to a church. 'This is St James – our Island church. I christen dere, I confirm dere, I married dere. Dis is de postcard of our church.'

'OK, OK. It's time for your tea,' I reply. I'll ask about your pension.'

When it comes to questions about the old people's money, no one ever gives information. There is no proper system of accounting, no questions can be asked and no one knows what becomes of the amounts which should be paid to inmates each week. It is still so. It always will be so. Grandpa's money was kept in a plastic envelope in a tin and then it silently vanished.

As the autumn deepens and the days grow colder more of the aged fall ill and are taken to the hospital. Few ever return. They do not struggle for life. It is a simple process of occupying space, sometimes briefly, sometimes for a substantial period, and then vacating it slowly, quickly, suddenly – even reluctantly. Relatives are told of deaths. Some are too busy to care, others too embarrassed to ask questions. To 'put away' old relatives leaves feelings of shame and guilt.

Christmas is approaching. Some of the inmates will be taken shopping – by bus to Harrods. It's a big day for them. They think they will see the Queen shopping there! Grandma and Grandpa do not want to spend money and nothing Adijah or I say can make any difference. My parents too have given up trying to influence my grandparents. The conditions in which they live often encourage this stubbornness in addition to confusion and helplessness.

The old people do not like the shortening days. Grandma in particular misses the birds and is sad that the ducks on the nearby pond are flying away. There is no more sitting out in the garden. But my grandparents notice the soft, muted colours of the evening skies. The sunsets are breathtaking. The sun is crested with crimson rays like a bird with plumes of fire on its head. But to see the sunsets one must stand at the window. Old people are not allowed to do this. They are expected to sit and watch TV, rock and drink tea.

At night the heavy curtains obscure sight and sound, emphasising the absence of a familiar fireplace – for there is no friendly, warming fire. There are radiators everywhere.

Yesterday my grandparents burnt coal, that leapt and flamed and danced like devils in the hearth. We often sat, Goldberg and I, waiting for the chestnuts we placed near the fire to be cooked. Then we would get the tongs and ask Grandma to remove the chestnuts and shell them for us. They tasted delicious. Goldberg liked to show off because he had lived on the Island and talked about the corn-cobs that were roasted in the yard on moonlit nights.

'We used to wait for the moon to rise and the shadows to gather. Then out would come the wood to make the blaze. When the blaze was gone and the coals glowed like crabs' eyes on a dark night, we would roast the corn. When it was done, our hands and teeth would work for hours. Everything would be hot and sweet.'

I miss Goldberg, truly, and the sight of a fire brings him to mind as he was in life. It is not possible to imagine him here in the home sitting beside my grandparents and talking to them.

In spite of the steady heat from the radiators, my grandparents complain of the cold.

Soon it will be the season of good will and the caregivers would like those old people who have relatives willing to accommodate them to be taken home. They are given instructions as to how to bring this about. 'Be sad when you see your family. Cry and they'll take you home for Christmas.' The caregivers are determined to enjoy themselves at this time, not that they don't for most of the year. They select new admissions on the principle of least trouble at Christmas, or so it seems.

Today Grandma has given me her large bag to take care of yet again. This is the third time she is entrusting her valued possession to me. It is already at home but she insists that I should go and fetch it for George to see. He is not around, however, having gone off to the Hayward Gallery. There is no music before lunch. The line of men and women walk silently to their places – indifferent to the act of eating. They complain loudly. 'We are not hungry. All you do in this place is eat. Food is not all we want. We want fun. Oh, where is George?' The caregivers shrug. 'You better be grateful else we'll send you lot to Ethiopia. What is skinny and walks on two legs?'

'Don't know,' come the whispered replies.

'Well, I'll tell you. An Ethiopian chicken!'

Nobody laughs. The old people have forgotten what a chicken is like and cannot recall who or what is Ethiopia.

Grandma and Grandpa sit silently side by side. They glance backwards and wave at me – the last vestige of their security, their link between past and present. They look frail and childlike as I did once. The thought of the childminder comes into my mind.

'Tyrone,' Grandma calls. 'Tek me home. Dis morning I look out and I see a hedgehog.' I suddenly feel liquid inside, and I stand still. I go to my car but cannot drive off.

I loiter around and eventually spend some more time with them. We leaf through the album. George has returned and soon joins us, beginning to talk of his Uncle Hartman who had a piano named after him because he was such a fine scale-maker. His mother is more wonderful than ever before and it was such a pity that both his sisters had died, one in babyhood and the other at eighty years of age. Grandpa too talks of his sisters. All he can ever say about them is that 'dey was two ugly people'.

Grandma is more settled now. I am free to go. I ask myself whether she really saw a hedgehog or was simply recalling those that lived in her garden and were fed each day on meat and bread. Grandma thought of them as her children. She talked to them, prayed on their behalf and told them of her problems with the developers.

When Grandpa had taken me to the library, out I had come with a book all about hedgehogs to help me with my school project. I had set about the project with a will and later it had won the prize of a picture book. My gran had placed it in the centre of the dining table so that we could all read the inscription:

> Tyrone Grainger
> Best Project Prize – Form 1Y

Is she now reminding me of that? I do not know. I cannot know.

As I watch TV that night this memory keeps recurring but Adijah is with me and I do not speak of it. We play some music to which we slow-dance. Then we love each other and as we lie so close together it is as if we etch our names on each other's heart. Her patience with my grandparents means so much to me and they feel safe and secure with her. I would have liked to confine her inside my heart, like a rare and beautiful gem, before the party season starts again. Her sound-system is heavily booked. I do not particularly care for her brother and partner, since he monopolises her during the time they work. My policy has always been to keep my friends close and my enemies closer but my prospective brother-in-law is neither friend nor foe. We had fought once at a cricket match, long ago, when we were children. I won the fight and he has never forgiven me. We strenuously avoid each other and I find that is the only way I can cope with him.

CHAPTER NINE

There is a Christmas tree in the lounge at The Birches and it is dressed like the dog's dinner. Its lights blink deceitfully and the baubles advertise their artificial beauty. There are presents for the inmates – boxes of tissues for the men and boxes of chocolates for the women. My grandparents have no taste for the present particularities of Christmas.

Yesterday it was different. Preparations for Christmas started early in our family. The tree was the high point of the preparations and we were consumed with excitement when it was brought in. We always spent Christmas with my grandparents. My parents helped to prepare the food – a variety of highly spiced roast meats, cakes and other good things. We all had new clothes because the Saviour was coming into our home. Grandpa always worked late, stitching, pressing and folding the clothes. And when the last order was collected he would close the door of his workroom in the loft and come downstars 'to his home'.

Excitement, pleasure and an anticipation of well-being and enjoyment seemed to be so tangible one could grasp them. My brother and I would sniff and shake and feel the parcels under the tree as we attempted to identify our presents, but everything was so securely wrapped that we were no wiser. We were showered with gifts and there was always a sense of anti-climax when Christmas disappeared without a trace and the tree, disrobed at last, looked stark and desolate.

Grandpa used to show us Christmas pictures of his Island which he kept in the album. There was the altar of St James's Church with its flowers and candles, as well as the crib crowded with angels and animals made of paper and cardboard. He said,

'When I was a boy I use to get a sixpence, an apple and a balloon from Father Christmas. Mother New Year give me a shirt or a pair of pants. You get toy, Tyrone, plenty toy. My sisters use to get baby-doll. I remember a nice dougla* one come in from Barbados. We never have a real Christmas tree. We either have a paper one or a bamboo branch decorate with dis and dat.'

Christmas day this year is bright but the sunshine is without heat. I leave home to fetch my grandparents. There are people about the streets, some walking dogs, while late revellers are staggering home. There are Asians in saris shopping with unconcern for the festive season. It is quiet at The Birches. At nine o'clock the old people are not yet astir except of course my Grandma who is in one of her moods. She does not want to spend Christmas day with us. This morning she thinks she would rather not see my mother and recalls some twenty-year-old misdemeanour in which my mum had figured. As a consequence Gran reacts with solid hostility and my father groans at the sight of her face when at last we arrive. This sound has an electrifying and unifying effect on everyone. When we are all clustered round him, in the comfort of his home, his asthma disappears and he eats a mince-pie or two. Grandma's little bag is stuffed with incidental food and she has spilt its contents several times since she came. Grandpa is reading a tract that a visiting Jehovah's Witness gave him, I believe. He is so engrossed that I am compelled to look over his shoulder. It is in fact page three of yesterday's *Mirror*, complete with nubile girl. He continues to 'read' the page and says with a smile, 'It is a religious tract. She is a nice young girl!'

Adijah has arrived and we eat our lunch. It is a simple one and we are content. We open our presents with cries of Happy Christmas to each other. Grandpa at once puts on his light-blue cardigan and Grandma matches him. My mother draws the curtains, lights some candles and we get ready to sing some carols.

Grandpa shouts, 'I want "While Shepherds . . .".'

*dougla: mix of East Indian and black.

'No,' shouts Grandma. ' "Once in Royal . . .".'

We have both. Grandpa throws himself into the singing while Grandma insists that George should come and play the piano. It is pointless to say that George is four miles away and that we don't have a piano. After a few more carols, mince-pies, cake and ice-cream are served. Everyone is in a stupor and dozes off.

'I never knew food was like Valium,' jokes Adijah. 'I feel sleepy.'

'Don't go to sleep yet. We have to take them back to The Birches.'

Inside The Birches there is activity and jollity. Candles are lit. Carol singers from the local church have come to help the old folk celebrate Christmas. There is more festive food – uneaten piles of it everywhere! But the caregivers are busy passing more around. They are in harmony with their charges. It is a kind of Bacchanalia. The ecstasy of doing good at Christmas is like a scar on the faces of the caregivers. There is a lightness of step, a free-flowing camaraderie. Now it is the time to love. It is Christmas day and it is nearly over. The disappearing hours goad the caregivers into a frenzy of generosity. They are as happy as dogs in a park. Everyone is. Happiness means having and sharing food and drink. Yes, everyone is under the claw of happiness. The floodgates of love are open – fully open.

I greet the Matron, and ask after George.

'He has gone to his relatives,' she says. 'He won't be back before Monday. His nephew's family are very good to him. He often goes out.'

'My gran is lost without him.'

'Well, I'll give her some chocolates and cheer her up.'

My heart sinks. Gran's small bag is already stuffed with dozens of uneaten chocolates.

'Come along, Tyrone,' Adijah calls. 'You haven't visited my mum's yet. There's more food waiting for you.' And she laughs heartily.

My heart sinks into my boots. 'Oh God,' I say. 'Please grant me the will to resist food. It should be rationed at Christmas. The eatingest time of the year.'

72

Adijah is still laughing and it seems as if her laughter will outlast the season.

But Christmas is over and the old routine descends upon us all like a cloud. The old people are once more seeking out lost possessions. From her chair Belladora accuses everyone of theft. Visitors come and go and George's mother is still a virtuous woman. God does not exist and he still believes in Man who finishes at death. Adijah and her brother are working a twenty-five-hour day. I tease her about making her first million by next Christmas. I spend a lot more time at the home and with my grandparents. As long as I appear, life at The Birches is tolerable for them.

A priest has begun to visit. Some recognise him as a priest but others see him as a schoolmaster, Santa Claus and even an estate agent. He distributes benign leaflets advertising church activities. Sometimes Grandma invites him to pray with her. Grandpa smiles behind his pipe. With the passing of time, their life has become something even they could understand and they are sailing on calmer waters – at least for the moment.

Grandpa has received another letter from Julietta. As soon as I arrive he says, as he always does, 'Read it, Tyrone. You eyes younger dan mine.'

> Dear Simon,
> I take up my pen in hand to tell you about Lucinda and to find out about your health and Clara. Sorry you missed the wedding but it in the middle of turning sour. Lucinda had put heart inside it but she say McBernie want too much although she never said what. He gone home to Scotland and she getting divorce. It's a shame that the marriage never last. But McBernie is a vexatious man.
> Love Julietta
> PS: Love to Clara, and to Tyrone, and to your son and wife, and to you, my dear friend and cousin, Simon.

73

I feel sad that the marriage has died so soon. By all accounts they were in love, and Lucinda was sure that God had pointed a finger at her life and opened a path for Mr McBernie, an elderly prisoner coming to the end of his sentence, whom fate had thrown into the same room with her dressed in her pink nylon nightie. 'He fell for the nightgown,' she had said, 'and then for my hair. I always got nice hair.' Adijah also feels sorry for Lucinda, who in her search for love gathered clouds that quickly turn stormy. She talks only of people who loved her but never discloses whom or what she loved. Love is received but never given in her world.

I ask Grandma about Belladora who always sits alone, a reservoir of sarcastic or aggressive remarks. Her brow is deeply furrowed, her fists clenched, her mouth a long, thin, unsmiling cut. All the cameras in her mind point backwards to suffering and a need for revenge.

Grandma replies, 'She gone to hospital. Dey cut off her foot. Dey makin' a false foot for her. She tell me so. She say she goin' to try it on and kick the Matron and all.'

Belladora's chair looks emptier than ever. Like her it seems to know what had been stolen and what had not.

The wind blows chill and little flecks of snow fall against the windows. George begins to play a Mozart sonata and silence settles like dust upon us all. Christmas has gone, and taken other associations with it. The snow has come and that too will soon be gone. The months flow by like a stream – sometimes clear, sometimes clouded.

Suddenly Adijah comes into my thoughts. I haven't seen her for what we call a week. We have our own calendar which measures minutes in hours, days in weeks, months in years. Our friends think us mad. I have not in fact, seen her for a day. She is busy with the disco and I look forward to the time when we can free ourselves of our responsibilities and marry each other. I miss her so much I telephone her home.

'She won't be back till early morning,' her mother says. 'She is playing at a birthday party in Streatham.'

'Have you the address?'

She gives it to me and I promise to meet Adijah there after the party. I do not know the people and I never gatecrash parties. I decide to collect her at about one o'clock in the morning, which is early for a party.

As fate decrees, my father has a full-blown attack of asthma after a fierce argument with Mum and has to be rushed to hospital. It is nearly twelve o'clock when I take my mother home, console her a little and then go off to meet my girlfriend.

The run through London is easy. The city lies sprawled but wide-awake in some places and half-asleep in others. I drive slowly, my thoughts moving from my life, to my parents' lives and then to those of my grandparents. Are we facing the same difficulties? Would we always do so? What qualities do I need to survive? Persistence, resilience, patience? I do not know.

Everything about the night seems larger, stronger, with even the shadows showing a sturdier quality. The very noise of life seems more sustained and spirited, the stars more numerous, the clouds denser. For some reason I feel small in the vast space that is London. I feel a foreboding on that articulate night so full of familiar sights and sounds. Destiny is abroad and stalking me like a jungle cat.

I find the street and turn into it. I can see people dancing close. I park and watch them. Not far from me young couples argue and bargain and giggle, while others grasp opportunity where it knocks. Everyone sounds vibrant and happy. The music stops and starts again. Hips sway to a soca. I can see Adijah at the first-floor window, selecting records and passing them to her brother Dante. It seems to be the last dance, a medley of pieces.

And then there is a terrific sound of breaking glass and fire and flames intermingle with screams of terror. The flames split into strands which seize and devour anything in their path, as if guided by a devilish intelligence. The house burns freely and resolutely. I can see silhouettes of writhing bodies engulfed with flames. I run to the house calling for Adijah but there is only the impenetrable darkness of thick smoke.

'Jump, Adijah!' I yell. 'Jump!'

People scream and hurl themselves out of windows but there is no escaping.

'Adijah!' I shout. 'Jump! Jump! Adijah!'

There is no answer. The fire-engine wails in the distance. The police arrive. Between them they keep back crowds and try to quench the fire. People desperately scream the names of their children – all from the black community.

I am in a frenzy. I run from police to firemen and back again, talking, asking, crying, begging to know.

'Where, Adijah, are you? Where are you?' My answer is the crackling, engulfing flames and dense earth-coloured smoke. I am aware only of my anguish. They have by now got the fire under control and firemen have begun to bring out the dead. Police are talking to the guests, asking their names, compiling lists, comforting the anguished.

'Oh, my God, Adijah! Adijah!' I lie on the grass and scream at the world. The night is suddenly colder, chilled by the spirits of those who have died. And then it comes back to me. A group I had seen huddled in a gather of shadows; those men gleefully savouring the destruction, who are they? I had glimpsed their hard, eager faces as they watched the ordeal of these people who to them were unbelonging and had to be destroyed. I ask myself again and again, why, nearly forty years after the coming of my grandparents to this land that was the source of their beliefs about life and civilised living, people burn others, deny others' capacity to feel and applaud their terror and their death.

I don't know how I get home but there I am when I regain my sanity a week later. Even so, I live in a kind of half-daze with Adijah's name constantly on my lips. I can vaguely make out faces – my mother's, hers, my father's, hers, and my Gran's. I don't know how long I lie there, afraid to return from my dungeon of pain and look life in the eye. Then one day as I hover between light and darkness, I overhear my parents talking. I listen, not meaning to. I hear not meaning to hear.

'It would take months, years even,' says my mother. 'Adijah jumped but she was still badly burnt on her hands and legs. Her head too, I believe. There will have to be plastic surgery, skin grafts, the lot.'

'Poor Adijah,' says my dad. 'As for Tyrone, looks like he too going to Mama Kane, the state he's in.'

I jump out of bed.

'Oh God! Adijah is alive. Alive! My own, dear Adijah.'

I begin to sob uncontrollably from relief and rekindled hope. 'I must see her,' I say. 'I must. God be praised.'

The hospital to which Adijah was admitted is nearer to Lurline's house and each day she obligingly telephones with news of Adijah. 'She bandaged up like a spaceman, burn bad. She got to have a lot of surgery on her arms and legs,' Lurline says in answer to my probing questions. 'I never see somebody burn like that. Thank God is not me.'

'When can I see her?' I ask. 'Will you find out?'

'As soon as they take the bandage off her head and face, I expect. All you can see now is holes for her eyes and nose, and a lot of bandage.'

I learn too that her brother Dante had also jumped from a window and, apart from minor burns, singed hair and a broken leg, he is all right. He sits a housebound casualty, grieving for his sister, their twelve dead young friends and for the others who have been hurt. I remember the killing eyes of the racists on that morning of my grandparents' eviction. Is this another of their crimes?

The whole community is in a state of shock and sorrow. Parties are cancelled for fear of further burnings. Young people suffer haunting nightmares of the fire. Parents weep in anguish over the sudden and cruel death of the children they love. Some were burnt alive, others choked to death by deadly smoke from furnishings when the bomb thrown into the house exploded in a fury of destruction. Marches and meetings do nothing to ease the grief. The police in their investigations flit from person to person like flies trying to find an exit from a carcass. The enquiries will go on for months – long after the inquests were held and the young people who were born here and died here have to be buried here. 'We know how they died, whatever the results of the enquiries,' their parents sob.

As the days pass I grow stronger, helped by the knowledge that Adijah has been spared. There is good and happy reason to go on living. I have not been allowed to see her because of the fears and stress that still torment her. I resume my visits to The Birches. Grandma is beside herself with joy. At first she cannot speak for weeping.

She chokes, 'I t'ink you dead, Tyrone. I ask God to help me bear it – another one for Mama Kane.'

Grandpa too greets me. He says nothing. His throat trembles with feeling and the tears in his eyes shine like glass beads. After a long time he sighs and in a timorous voice whispers, 'Blessed be the ties dat bind our heart in human love.' Then he shakes me fiercely by the hand and sits me down.

A lot has changed at the home. Belladora had died in hospital and had been buried but her artificial foot arrived after that undistinguished event. Matron found that someone had lovingly dressed it with Belladora's ankle sock and shoe, and now she keeps it in her office.

Belladora had been a singer and dancer but never reached the heights nor earned the rewards she deserved. Now it is as if she still sits in her chair glowering at those who come too close. I can still hear her snarling her request for the 'Lambeth Walk' whenever George said sweetly, 'And now your choice, Belle.'

George too looks thinner and more subdued. He has a pain in his chest, he says, and hates the thought of going back to hospital yet again. Shortly before his admission to The Birches, he had cataracts removed from both eyes. I watch him as he walks towards the garden door. He seems to be in great pain, preferring to tuck it away in his body like a coin in his purse.

'No music today, George,' calls another new entrant. A tiny man with a neat goatee. George shakes his head and goes on. I walk towards the little man to introduce myself.

'Don't talk to him,' says Dolly, the old woman who looked as if bits of her died in the day and were reconstituted at night. 'Don't talk to him. He's a child-molester. I knew him before. Honest. He is a child-molester. God help us all in here!'

George turned round and laughed heartily – his beard looked like striped wool in the slit of sunshine that showed through the curtain.

'Really, Dolly, you're not a child – but a lovely, generous woman who hates to gossip.'

George plucked a plastic tulip from the vase and gave it to her, and she went happily into the lounge.

Charlie, the old man with the goatee, found a seat and began reading a book.

The Matron walks by. I tell her how sorry I feel about Belladora and all the others who leave her with such regular suddenness. She nods and then replies, 'When you get to our age, death becomes a certainty. What is sad is when the young get knocked down. The old don't mind dying.'

'My girlfriend just missed it,' I say.

'I heard. And all those young people. God help us. When will we all learn? Have you seen your girlfriend yet?'

'No, each day I hope. But she wants no one to see her in her present state. She's a proud, intelligent girl.'

'Well, it isn't only the body. It's also spirit, also heart and mind and soul that has to heal,' she whispers, as she pats my arm. 'All must heal.' Then abruptly she walks away. Minutes later she returns with Belladora's foot cradled in her arms like a baby.

'Isn't this good,' she croons. 'Excellent craftsmanship. I wonder how she would have got on with it.'

The Matron pauses for a moment, reflecting on her dead friend. 'I knew her for years – we grew up in the same street,' she volunteers. 'She was bitter to the end, you know. She often talked about the home she grew up in, abandoned by her mother, mistreated by everyone.'

'If you cringe you get kicked,' I reply, tersely. 'That's what happens, like it or not.'

The Matron does not appear to have heard me and runs on, her voice now sharp enough to shave my head.

79

'At school poor Belle endured years of torment, but she just wept and complained to the teachers.'

'Why didn't she fight back?' I ask.

This time the Matron registers what I say. 'She could not fight,' she responds. 'She grew up fast, worked in a munitions factory and then got married – to Tom Widgeley, who was in the navy.'

'That must have made a difference to her,' I suggest. 'Someone to be at peace with while the war raged outside.'

'Yes,' snaps the Matron. 'Briefly. Two trips and then Tom's ship was torpedoed and he was gone. Her mother didn't want to know her. She'd done well for herself and didn't welcome the living proof of her descent into the black world.'

'Don't blame the mother,' I retort, determined not to accept Belle's circumstances as a pass to unhappiness. 'A khaki-coloured kid was a blot on the escutcheon in those days. What would you have done?'

The Matron is silent for a while. Something – a sensation, a memory perhaps – shows on her face like a stain. It is as if she is rearranging the pages of her own life.

Suddenly she blurts out, 'I married during the war. A Jamaican airman. And when peace came I settled in his homeland. I'm no stranger to prejudice or insult. After my husband died I was on my own. Friendless. The tainted white widow of a black Jamaican. Belle was a half-caste. I was an outcast.'

'Those were hard times,' I say, 'but no one pretended they were better. My grandfather was out there with nothing but his courage and his cunning, his desperation and his hopes. Nothing more. He found places of rest in his life!'

'Oh yes, there was the pretence,' she counters. 'They condemned us while they talked of Empire, while their daughters flocked round American servicemen, yelling, "We love our coloured sweethearts!" '

She is now weeping quietly as she mourns her vanished youth and her lost love.

I feel confused. An avalanche of feelings sweeps down on me.

80

The silence speaks deeply to both of us, till I venture, 'You know what Bob Marley said?'

She nods. 'Trust God and grow wise.' She whispers, 'We'll all be wiser one day.'

CHAPTER TEN

It is three long months before I am allowed to visit my Adijah. She sits in a chair, a distant, unseeing look in her eyes. I had expected to see many more disfiguring burns on her face and am relieved when I see that the damage has confined itself to one area alone. Her singed hair has grown back but there are marks on her neck and arms. Her skin looks frighteningly tender where its naturally warm brown colour had been seared by the heat. The nurse assures me that in spite of appearances Adijah is not in pain.

'People in pain toss and turn, but she is calm,' she explains. 'If only we could persuade her to speak, Mr Grainger. Not a word has passed her lips since she's been in here. At night she wakes up screaming and the terror in her eyes is something to behold. It is as if she has found a safe place inside herself, where nothing of the tragedy is known. And there she has stayed.'

I take her hand in mine and whisper her name but she looks straight ahead as if her ears and eyes have been touched by the devil. The darkest thoughts come into my mind. Has the heat of the inferno in which she had been caught destroyed some vital part of her hearing?

'Adijah!' I call again. 'Can you hear me?' Apart from a slight flickering of her eyelids and the emergence of the tiniest of smiles she simply stares straight ahead. A dagger goes through my heart, but I continue to talk of the good times we have shared and music we love. A tear slowly trickles down her face, and her hand grasps mine as if, like a fledgling, its very life depends on clinging to its perch. I think that she should be discharged and later I voice this to her parents.

'She would be among her own,' I say, 'eating what she likes and sleeping in her own bed.' Her mother agrees and Adijah is discharged the following week. After that she improves rapidly, still silent and shut in, but obviously enjoying our walks.

Spring is on the way. The trees have begun to show leaf. Everything is awakening and stirring to the wind and weather. The air is fresh with a kind of gentle touching and stroking of all God's creatures. Blackbirds fly with twigs and grass in their beaks.

We visit my grandparents at The Birches. Although Adijah is troubled and frightened, she still loves going out. Her youth is her hope and her strength. I play snakes and ladders with my grandparents while she turns the pages of the album. Her enjoyment of the sepia-coloured photographs is clear. It is as if the destruction of the fire has given a new dimension to her understanding of permanence. And then one day a simple yet extraordinary thing happens.

A large black cat known at The Birches as Dandy jumps over the fence carrying a dead pigeon in his mouth. Dandy sits in one particular spot to devour his birds and on that day Adijah has usurped the spot. He reclaims it by jumping on her with such force that his claws pierce her leg. Her scream so terrifies him that he drops the bird. She has never been a lover of cats, especially of those carrying dead birds. She stares at the dishevelled feathers, the chewed and bleeding wing, the half-opened eyes and beak and she screams her revulsion with a latent terror.

'Are you hurt?' I ask anxiously.

'No,' she manages to whisper. 'The bird was! It's dead! Dead! The heat is still in my face. The bird! It's dead!'

'There! There!' I say, cradling her in my arms. 'It's a bird! Cats kill birds!'

She starts to scream again. The Matron runs out with some of the caregivers. They watch bewildered as I lead her away. I seat her in the car and after she stops sobbing I return to my grandparents.

'Everything OK?' I ask. Grandpa nods. 'See you tomorrow. I

must go.' Grandma strokes the air contemplatively. 'Goodbye, Tyrone,' she says. 'Goodbye.'

After that incident Adijah begins to speak but for some considerable time afterwards her voice frightens her. Even as she speaks she looks about her as if trying to find the source of the sound. We seek the help of an experienced therapist who, through patience and encouragement, helps her towards regaining her old strengths; but neither her vivacity nor her voice is the same as before. She seems to trust no one and shies away from strangers.

Dante, housebound with leg and hip injuries, is delighted with her progress, and in a way relieved with the news that his dead friends have been identified and buried. There is a harsh backbone of pain and loss within the community. People know that the dead do not return but they are always on the lips of those who knew and loved them. My grandparents have seen bad times but our so-called better times are brutal. There is no picture in the album to compare with those that have been taken of the ruins, of the house that has been razed, of Adijah swathed in bandages or of Dante racked with pain. There is none to match the faces of parents whose children have been laid waste, or the sorrow of those that mourn the Streatham Twelve – all young martyrs to xenophobia and hate.

My love for Adijah deepens with her suffering and I long for the time when we can marry and take care of each other and of the children we will have. When I look at her striving to remember the time before the flames, or to hear the echoes and voices of the past, I am overcome with grief. The vision of the raging flames, the smell of burning and the plaintive wailing of ambulances fill me with hostility to the whole world. My old friends in The Birches sense the change in me even though they cannot understand the community loss. George is the most sympathetic. The wars he has survived have taught him brotherhood. He knows that sorrow knows no creed nor colour.

'I told you,' he says, 'Mother had a black lodger before the war. He was very polite. And as for fires, I've seen them aplenty, during the war. One night London was a mass of flames – bombs falling like rain. We went to this house – all that was left of it. It was little less than a hole in the ground. All that we found was a lovely Chinese vase and a woman's shapely hand. The fingers were beautifully manicured.' He smiles self-consciously. 'The Jerries were fascists and look where they are now. But bad people never learn good. And we must never think they do.'

'It must have been a terrible time,' I say.

'Yes, but we did not give in. We kept fighting on. You can't let the likes of them get the better of you. Bad 'uns hold together in deeds. Good friends are always together in spirit. And you must have heard of the old bulldog, Winston Churchill! He led us to victory.'

The next day George is too ill to get up and later that week he is moved to New End Hospital. I visit him and find him surrounded by relatives, listening to a concert on the radio with him. I am struck by the quality of their affection for him. They leave when I show up but I can sense his pleasure that they have come.

'Whose music?' I ask.

'Gounot,' he replies. He knows and will love the composers of fine music to the end of his days.

A priest is silently comforting the dying. He warily edges past George's bed.

'Do you want him to come?' I ask.

'I'm on my way out and I don't need his help. Thank God for that!' He tries to laugh but pain chokes off whatever little strength is left in him.

'Don't you believe, even now?'

'God is never around when clouds threaten and storms break out. He's in heaven in comfort and stays there till it's all over.'

I nod.

'Sing something,' he says. 'Anything.'

'If I sing they will put me in Broadmoor,' I reply.

'Champagne Charlie is my name,' he sings – or tries to sing as he gasps for breath between the words.

Two hours later he dies.

News of George's death greatly affect my grandparents. Adijah too feels saddened. She has greatly loved the old man. As she talks of him and repeats his stories, her voice seems to come from a reservoir of sadness somewhere inside her.

On the day of the cremation the chapel of the crematorium is full. Even the Matron and some of the ever-changing caregivers can temporarily cease their plundering of the aged and attend, although they are not invited. The same ubiquitous priest who had been visiting the hospital conducts the service. I overhear a relative telling him that the old man died an unbeliever and asking that his comments be more secular than religious. He agrees, but turns out to be a bird with only one song.

George had wanted none of the trappings of mourning but asked that 'a flower in season be provided for everyone who came to put him down'. The old organist plays a Chopin nocturne, and then comes the oration.

'We are here to celebrate the passing of our brother in Christ, George, whom we remember as a good man and a Christian. We commend him to heaven and to the everlasting arms of He who died for our sins. George was a devout and living disciple of our Lord and cleansed from his sin may he find everlasting life in the arms of his saviour and eternal peace in heaven.'

Not content with that, he asks us to sing 'Onward Christian Soldiers'. Since few know it, he sings it alone.

It is too much for us who knew George as a convinced and hardened atheist. Our choked sniggers turn into a flood of laughter. There are visions of him fighting his way out of the everlasting embrace and spurning discipleship of any kind, however well intentioned. He was an independent man, free of religious beliefs, and was a good man, secure in the virtues he wanted to cultivate. The infectious laughter grows louder and spreads. Self-restraint goes to the four winds as laughter peals through the chapel. The confused priest looks round about and up and down, as much as to ask in biblical terminology, 'Whence cometh all this mirth?' He clears his throat and then coughs us to silence. 'Let us pray,' he barks, his voice full of the authority of habit.

He races into the burial service. Even my grandparents can't keep up with him. As George slides away I feel what must be sorrow. At the loss of my brother I felt shock, and unfairness. I feel the pain of brotherhood for the twelve that died at Streatham, but this is a new and momentarily liquefying feeling. Yet we leave the chapel pleased that we have celebrated George's passing in a moment of laughter – rather like the applause which followed his performances on the piano. The sun shines as we each receive our sprig of wallflower. 'What a lovely day!' he would have said.

Suddenly Dolly begins to sing, 'After the ball was over'. Everybody hums the tune. I hum something as I do not know the song. Adijah squeezes my hand. 'I can't sing. I'm full of some feelings I cannot name.' Grandma and Grandpa throw themselves into the singing as they did when, treble and alto, they sang in the choir of their village church. I kiss them goodbye and walk away towards my car. They are going back in Matron's car. But there are footsteps behind me. I turn and see Charlie. He holds out one of Grandma's coins.

'The old lady dropped this. I think it might be valuable. It's got a galleon on one side and some peculiar markings on the other. It might be worth something. If I was you I should find out.'

'Thank you, Charlie. She's always had them. None of us paid them any mind. It's only since they sold their house that the coins have surfaced again.' I hold the coin for a moment and drop it in my pocket.

Grandma had brought over to England several bits and pieces that had been left to her mother. Her grandfather, a man of some culture, used to buy oddments from plantation sales, but Grandma never mentioned him. She always told us that her father had given her the coins and she had kept them to remember him. He had never said they were worth anything and it had never occurred to her to think otherwise. In her saner days she had once said that in a house on the Island an African prince lived long ago. He had been banished there by the British overlords. He was incredibly rich and left money on the Island. I treated it as a fairy tale.

The next day I ask Grandpa about what Grandma calls her doubloons.

'Dey no good,' he affirms. 'She always had dem.' And that is that. I question her again.

'I had plenty but I can't remember where I put dem – some been in my big bag,' she replies. 'Dey counterfeit.'

When I go home I tip out the contents of her bag. It is a most sick-making experience. The bag contains the usual bric-a-brac that old women carry but the thread and thimbles have become entangled with bits of ancient fruit and encrusted with chocolate and other snacks that Grandma has 'saved for later'. There are shoes, ancient religious tracts, the earth she used to carry now overtaken with fungus and one of Goldberg's socks stuffed with toy cars. It all smells as if a whiff of it could eliminate an army. I hurriedly mask my nose and go on looking. But try as I may there are no coins to be found. I have packed some of Grandma's possessions in our loft and I decide to look among them.

I spend several hours emptying boxes and at last come upon her trunk. She had travelled to this country by boat and had brought with her several things from her grandfather's communally owned plantation house that subsequently fell prey to rot and woodworm. There is nothing of interest except a dirty picture about two foot by eighteen inches. It shows a group of peasant women and children wearing horrid masks and is signed Jose – I can't figure out the rest. I hate the picture but I take it downstairs intending to place it before Grandma in order to get its story.

When I show it to her she points to an old man in the album and says how wicked he was. Her mother told her that while his family starved he went around the Island plantations buying and selling objects that took his fancy. He was a great traveller and after his death nobody talked about him except to say he was a no-good money-waster.

Unexpected events are to follow the discovery of that painting. I decide to take it to the British Museum Picture Section and they say it is of importance and that I should have it cleaned and insured. I have no money to do either but manage to borrow some from Adijah, who borrows some from Dante.

When the picture is cleaned it is austere in colour but poignant and dramatic. I then take it to a leading auctioneer and he identifies it as having been painted by Jose Gutierrez Solana (1886–1945), a Spanish artist and traveller to the West Indies. The picture is called *The Masks* and could be auctioned to my considerable advantage. The auctioneer enthuses about its harshness, its baroque quality, its tragic sense. I take both my parents and grandparents to see the restored and reframed picture. They decide that as it is so ugly it should be sold. We ask for seller anonymity and it is bought by a private collector for an enormous sum of money – more than I have ever dreamed of in my life. I shudder to think that my grandmother could have thrown the picture away or destroyed it, keeping it only as proof of the wastefulness of her ancestor.

After we receive the money my grandparents give me full control over it.

'You find worth, Tyrone. Control de money. De old man was bad. He use to spy. He was bad.'

Uncle Herod clarifies his 'badness' for me. Apparently the British had banished an African prince to the Island for having revolutionary thoughts and disobeying their edicts. The old man was put in charge of this arrogant prince and did not help him come to terms with his new life. Instead he filched all the prince's possessions. I understood then why nobody talked of John Vanette, reformed pirate, entrepreneur, roamer and beach-comber – a devious, brick-eyed man who robbed and plundered with impunity.

Mum and Dad decide at once to go home and take the old people with them now that they can afford to buy decent care. I broach the subject of going home head on.

Grandma, whom I thought would give me the most trouble, says yes straight away. But Grandpa, in his much more contemplative way, has reservations enough to fill ten thousand cricket pitches.

'All my friends dead and gone. Who dere for me? All dese year I make new foundation for my mind. I can't go back to de old ways. Over dere de eye of criticism like a torchlight on me! I know to work widout a boss. Yes, here people don't talk to you but dey let you be. Nobody never get lynch yet. I old now. All I want is food, clothes and a warm place to sit down.'

Finally he says that he doesn't want family. He had enough of them when he was young and, he continues, 'Everyt'ing free here. Every'ting free – de bus, de prescription, de pension. I never had money before, and it don't matter now.'

My heart is so full of sorrow it overwhelms me. I try to explain that nothing is free, and while there are no lynchings people are getting burnt and stabbed instead. He remains impervious to all counter argument. Only what has happened to him and his friends is valid. He is unrelenting and freeranging in his doubts, and after he has paused for breath he goes on, 'A lot of flies everywhere. No water closet. No bath, only shower. I forget how to manage t'ings like dat.'

I feel more depressed the longer he rants on. Here we are, not super rich like those who win the pools, but with more money than we could have made by selling four houses in 1984. I should be feeling elated. I try to recall a proverb or two about money – but all those that come into my head have to do with work, education or my parents. Proverbs such as 'Hard work is good medicine', or 'Education is power', or 'Never forget you come from God through your parents'. At this moment I would prefer to have come into this world on my own, or even through an incubator, like a chicken.

I should be adventurous, go out disco-dancing with my girl, but I reckon that there will be time to do these things. I tell myself that I can't neglect my grandparents. My father still expects me to stand by them even though my one year off will stretch into two.

My grandpa's words devastate me, however. And yet he keeps on. 'De food so full of oil. When I was boy, I eat rice-pap every Friday night, when de food run out. De bread so hard because dey mangle de dough, to get de raise out of it. Herod say it break up his teeth.' On and on he goes, relentlessly quoting idiot after idiot.

Grandma is the first to show talk-fatigue. 'Stay here, Simon,' she says. 'Leave here. Dey who God join together, goin' home will put asunder.'

Then something snaps inside me.

'Grandpa, how long've you been here? How old were you when you come?' I growl.

'Forty-something.'

'You live forty-something years in the Island. Child, boy and man. Now you're talking like you crawl out from under a stone – finding fault with everything. Every day I come, I talk to you. You say sell the picture, get the money – do this, do that! What do I get in return? Nothing. No appreciation! No thanks. No nothing! I'm fed up, Grandpa, fed up!'

'Mo' man refuse, mo' dinner serve,' says Grandma.

'I'm going home,' I snap. 'Dad has stopped getting up a posse to send after me for every little thing I do wrong. I'm going where I would get co-operation from my family.'

Grandpa clears his throat. 'Tyrone,' he wails. 'Come, Tyrone. Please come and talk.'

'No, Grandpa,' I say. 'No more talk. I have had enough. No more cool time! Action! Now!'

CHAPTER ELEVEN

In spite of my outburst I need a shoulder to cry on, and go in search of Adijah.

'I feel like a long holiday,' I say. 'The old people are getting to me. I am expecting too much, perhaps. Would you come with us if we go home? A year off should be good for you. It would be a little holiday for you.'

'I have got deferment,' she says. 'The authorities were most kind. My mum and dad wouldn't object if your parents are with us.'

I take her in my arms. She is warm and soft and rational. Her youth gives her a reassuring radiance yet it is frightening to think that in time we too could become grandparents, not only opionated and truculent but also reactionary and indifferent to our fate.

'Love is said to be a destructive emotion,' I muse, 'but it is life that is the most destructive of all.'

'I disagree,' she says. 'It's how you feel about love and life that either destroys or elevates. I love you, Tyrone. I hope we never grow too old to love in a healthy and ever-flowering way.'

That simple sentiment puts me back on course. With Grandpa and Grandma life is dying each day, bit by bit, until the last bit succumbs. I have a lot of living to do, and Adijah is prepared to chance it with me.

The daily visits to The Birches, the sporadic battles on their behalf, my pledge to my father to settle my grandparents in the home, have changed me completely. My life has slowly begun to feel as if it were being crushed under a slowly moving wheel, but now no more. Life is out there waiting for me. Adijah is here beside me. We make love tenderly, yet fiercely and with unspoken commitment. My grandparents are echoes of their time, we are the voices of ours.

When I see my grandpa again, I have so many things to say they very nearly choke me.

'You fought yesterday, Grandpa. On the streets of Notting Hill?' I ask with some bitterness. 'Why do you think the young people are fighting today in Brixton, Bradford, Sheffield, Bristol, elsewhere?'

Without a moment's hesitation he replies, 'Because dey is lazy and wicked.' Vehemently he adds, 'Ask Herod. He say dey smoke ganja and burn incense to hide de scent of de ganja. Dey don't care to work. Dey care to beg and mug people. Dey get too much free food in de school and dey not mannersable. Dey disrighteous. Dey never hungry like I was! Dey never know naked poorness.'

'Grandpa,' I reply. 'You and Herod turn old and ugly with age. I am one of the young ones. Look at me and bow down in shame before me. You're talking about me and my generation of young people.' I feel as if there is a merry-go-round ridden by ghouls in my head.

'You is different, Tyrone,' he says. 'You is family, you is we, me grandson. We put better t'ings inside you. Believe dat, Tyrone! Ask anybody.'

I shake my head. 'I am not a hologram. You are. Old age is the shadows. I am young. I am real. I know what I am. I'm glad that I am young and that the likes of Herod can't influence me.'

'I want to go home, Tyrone,' he wails.

'Don't worry, Grandpa. We will give you your share if you want to stay, then we will go. You don't care how strangers treat you. We do. You don't care what happens to you. We do. We're sorry to care for you, Grandpa. You see yourself as old. But time will come, when you're black and old. That will not be too bad. Herod will console you.'

'Tyrone, I goin' wid Clara,' he sobs. 'I goin' wid Clara. Clara is my wife.'

'Yes,' joined in Grandma. 'In a boat. Tyrone? We come in boat. We goin' in boat?'

'You're going in an aeroplane, Grandma,' I reply. 'It's much quicker.'

No one has ever influenced her the way Herod has influenced Grandpa. One part of her mind is flighty, the rest is as sound as new money. No wonder people love her. At that moment I feel closer to her than I feel to my mother. She is an enigma. One minute she seems so frail, another she is strong – even younger than my mother.

'Have you ever done anyone harm, Grandma?' I ask.

'Only you grandpa – once! I knock him wid a fry-pan. I aim for his head. I get his back.' We laugh long and loudly. It is nice to hear her laughter. There is a ring of hope in it.

We play chequers but our games are getting fewer. There is a simmering in Grandma and an uncertainty in Grandpa and more talk about going home. In spite of being forbidden to disclose our plans, they tell everyone. 'We goin' home wid Tyrone. We goin' to see de sun.' I am therefore forced to give formal notice of their departure.

The Birches is as excited as my grandparents and the VIP treatment they are being given is responsible for Grandpa's indisposition. He takes sick one night and fills every room with his moans. The doctor is summoned and so am I. He tosses and turns and the drops of sweat on his brow look like a ring of beads. I feel as if I have brought this about by the pressure I have put on him to think as I want him to.

'Doctor,' I say, 'I feel terrible about Grandpa. This is all my doing. I pressured him to decide before he was ready. If he dies, it would be because of me.'

'Die? He won't die. His heart is as strong as iron. What he should do is to refrain from putting so much lamb curry in his stomach!'

'Lamb curry?'

'Yes. Charlie apparently bought him a takeaway to help him cope with the food. He's worried about the food. He ate too much. He be OK tomorrow.'

It transpires that Grandpa has talked so much about the war which is about to take place between his stomach and the Island food that all his friends have decided to help him. Whatever condiment he has mentioned has been bought for him and this is beginning to take a toll of his system. My mother is seething with rage. She is sure Grandpa is being deceitful and manipulative. She is sure he is going to spoil her life. She is sure also that he has deliberately set about causing her husband's asthma attacks to increase.

My mother is a woman who thinks in extremes – no middle road for her. Grandpa is either a lion or a lamb, a butterfly or a wasp. I leave her to blow herself out like the tornado Grandma so often talks about. When my mum says, 'I'm going home. I was glad to come now I'm glad and ready to go back,' I know she is also ready for a cup of tea. I make her one. As she sips it she whispers, 'Tomorrow I'm collecting Goldberg from Mama Kane sure as God made morning.' She weeps bitterly for about ten minutes, blows her nose loudly and then resumes her ironing, her furies spent until another day.

Adijah lies asleep in my room. I slip out of the house for a while. I buy a local paper and as I open it two familiar faces catch my eye. Under the headline ELDERLY COUPLE RETURN TO CARIBBEAN are my grandparents. The writer says they have worked hard all their lives and have been given sheltered accommodation, but now an unexpected inheritance has made their return home possible. They are to be commended for the wonderful example they are setting to other elderly people of ethnic minority origins. The writer makes it clear he wants all old black people to follow my grandparents' example and go home. There is not a word about the eviction months before. I am so angry. I drive like a Jehu to The Birches. It transpires that it was not Matron but Charlie who has seen fit to call the papers.

'Charlie,' I say as calmly as I could. 'Why?'

'Well, we were 'appy for 'em. I wish I 'ad a 'ome to go to. They're celebrities for a day. What's the 'arm in that?' He smiles surreptitiously, his unlit pipe firmly clenched between his teeth.

'I could never stop getting my teeth into farts,' he adds contemplatively. 'I've always done it.'

Grandma and Grandpa take no interest whatsoever in the article in the evening paper, but the whole family turns up to find out about the inheritance – Julietta, Lucinda, Herod . . . everyone.

'No inheritance,' I explain. 'The pools. I come up! Been trying for years! I never thought my system would work.'

So they go home envious but happy for us, and they all promise to visit as soon as life and time allow. Herod had probed and questioned, his large flaps of ears quivering for information about the amount we have 'won', but I did not tell.

There is a farewell party at The Birches. Sometimes Grandma seems to be aware of what is happening, then suddenly she is at a party given for someone else. Grandpa seems to have grown shy. He feels he is doing something grievously wrong – betraying a lifelong acceptance of service to his country, betraying the destiny of suffering, betraying his ability to scream in silence and as a black man to be visible and invisible at the same time.

We all attend the party. It is the second time my father has visited The Birches. He was there when my grandparents entered the home and now again at their exit. Adijah, beautiful in red, forms a lovely backdrop to Matron's speech, a masterpiece of patronising clichés. But with tongue in cheek I thank her.

After that our preparations to leave become urgent and even frenzied at times. Some things have to be done quickly if we are to depart at a reasonable time of year. My parents leave their home for annual letting with an agency. The kind of tenants they want would be the ones most likely to purchase the house if they decide to sell. I think of Grandma's possessions in the attic. What else is there of value? I hope my parents will not sell their home and that at some point Adijah and I will live there and our children will play in that handkerchief of a garden, as I did.

96

On the morning of our departure, autumn has truly arrived. The year has come full circle and now it is as if the leaves, falling and whirling in the wind, are tearful to see us leave this land. Funnily enough I feel no regret, no pangs of sorrow. I live here yet I have no feelings about the place. I have always felt an outsider.

I never noticed affection such as is shown for my grandparents on the day of their departure. They have been cogs in a wheel, and set apart by their colour. At The Birches people become significant through death. My grandparents are significant and alive because some ancestor, long ago, had accidentally made this moment happen. Whatever he was, cut-throat or priest, black or white, his greed or his sense of beauty now reaches across the decades and touches my life.

Grandma climbs into the car. 'Goodbye,' she calls. 'I'm goin' home. I sendin' a bit of sun in a bottle for you. It name rum. It hot.' Grandpa merely waves and looks straight ahead.

Charlie runs out with a bouquet of flowers. 'This is your cut, Clara. They paid me twenty quid for your story – the papers I mean.' Grandma holds the bouquet close. Solitary faces peer from the windows. A hypocritical crowd of caregivers waves from the doors.

'I feel like a bride,' she says. 'I have orange blossom when I marry Simon in St James-the-Less Church. It nice in dere.'

The Matron rushes out waving a furry dog. 'Clara,' she shouts. 'Here you are. Cuddle it and think of us.'

'I don't want it,' Grandma shouts back. 'Dey got real dogs on de Island. Beside, I ent baby any more.'

'My gran is no longer a fruit-and-nut cake, Matron,' I tease.

We drive to the airport. Grandpa is silently weeping. Adijah comforts him by patting his shoulder. 'It ent de best but I get use to it,' he sobs. 'I remember de people. Dey all got ways. You get use to ways. Dere was George. A happy man. I use to de place and de people.'

'Never mind, Grandpa. You're going to your own,' I say. 'Everybody will be waiting for you.'

It begins to rain. The windows cloud over. Grandpa is asleep.

We finally reach the airport and check in and sit down to await our flight call.

'Do you think they're nervous?' Adijah whispers.

'No, they've been on planes before.'

Grandpa wakes up, reads his Bible and then begins to look through the album as if reacquainting himself with the people in it. Just as it is time to board, Herod, Lurline and their grandchildren arrive. Herod hugs Grandpa. 'If it got your name on it, boy, nothing you can do. You zip down and biff – a puff of smoke.'

'Herod, please,' I say.

'*Uncle* Herod!' he snaps. 'My name is for adults only. Not for a jumped-up fowl cock.'

'Uncle Herod, then. Can't you see Grandpa is upset?'

'Look, Tyrone. You Grandpa always upset. He never had no guts. He always upset. Nothing new.'

'You old bastard,' I hiss. 'Leave him alone. He's better off without you!'

We hurry away before he can recover.

'Herod always like dat,' Grandpa says. 'He full of crab-antics. He got to pull people down.'

I hug him. 'You're great, Grandpa. You're great. Ask anyone.'

But Herod has got through. On the plane Grandpa goes to the loo three times. Once for himself and twice for his nerves. Grandma sleeps so hard she misses her meals. My parents are in another part of the plane. My father, free of travel sickness this time, reads and smiles and waves at us. He drinks all his free drinks. I feel as if I have accomplished something, as if I have worth. I am not just Tyrone, the grandson. I am a man. I nestle beside Adijah. She pulls one of my locks.

'Do you still need these?'

'I don't know.'

'What do they do for you except make you sinister and peculiar? Why do you need sinister–peculiar? Nobody cares about you, black-man!'

'I care about me,' I reply.

'Indeed! I must avoid you.'

'I'm a man. I can take it. I'm a perfectly strong, active, virile man.'

'Is that so? Tell everybody.'

'I'm tired,' I say. 'And comfortable the way I am. I am also content.'

'Get over it.'

'Do you need a drink, sir?' asks the stewardess. 'And you, madam?'

'An orange for me,' I say. 'Thank you.'

'Just plain water, thank you.' Adijah gurgles the water and then reads her magazines.

Is she in love with me? I wonder. Really in love. No reservations. People must have reservations. They set limits for others. Maybe she should have some. She ends there, I begin here. I fall asleep but jump awake with the request to 'Fasten seat belts'. We have come home. It has taken many long hours of flying.

We have really come home. The people in the airport look like hundreds of multi-coloured ants – each pursuing some activity by sheer instinct. It takes us ages to clear Customs. The officers are not to be hurried and then, here we are.

Among the relatives gathered to meet us is a pretty girl – tall, slender and doe-eyed. She moves like a gentle fawn and smiles furtively every time our eyes meet.

'Who are you? I ask.

'I'm Stephy.'

'You are very attractive.'

'You girlfriend more attractive than me. I am not a London girl. I'm pure Island. You all staying long?'

'We have come home!'

'To this place. Everybody leaving this place. Even the boys who only use sugar cubes to dice with leaving this place.'

'Well, we'll see. I must get a taxi, actually two taxis.'

She goes off to help Adijah and Grandma. They are like old friends, talking and joking, and then everyone and everything is ready for the journey to Picktown. Our luggage alone is a dead giveaway. Old and young know that Picktown people have come home. The old wave to us as vigorously and eagerly as age allows, the young with the restraint of unfamiliarity. As yet they share no kind of experience with us, nor do they yet know the spectre that drove the traveller away from home. As we whip past a toothless old man yells, 'A bad home is better than a good abroad.'

'Yes,' says Grandma. 'No place like home. Be it ever so humble.'

Grandpa's quivering lips cannot support his pipe and he is forced to remove it, empty it and place it in his pocket.

CHAPTER TWELVE

As the taxis climb the steep hill that takes us out of the airport, the Island shines like a multi-coloured jewel, tranquil in the wisdom and design of nature. In the distance is the sea, reflecting the clear blue of the skies and the fluffiness of the clouds while it crawls up the sand to leave a delicate frill of surf. Small birds, their wings radiant in the sunlight, skim the waves. Not far from the shore, dull-grey cranes, gauldings to the Islanders, like one-legged statues, wait to spring to life and seize in their dagger-like beaks wandering crabs and fishes. Children seine close to the shores and make noise enough to be heard for miles. Trees and shrubs sheltering colonies of insects provide layers of shadows and quiet places where flowers grow in profusion.

No transient blooms of spring in this place, no unwilling summer, no wanton autumn with its magic tints. Green is the colour of this land – light green and dark, pale-green and sparkling. Picketing the sands are the coconut palms that sweep the air with their fronds, their nests of fruit high above the earth. I am delighted by the blend of sights, the clear sound of voices and the friendship and warmth about me.

A macadamised road links the villages, their peace rusted by the many buildings in the process of construction, and by the dull emptiness of new houses awaiting the bustle of occupation. The villages have been given exciting names like Widow's-Dip and Whortle Berry Bond.

'I 'member when dey name Widow-Dip,' Grandma says. 'I must be five or six year old. Mother Critchley use to sell fish down by dere but one day God make her see her two son and her

101

husband drown. She put brick in her pocket – then she swim out and dead in de sea.'

'What a way to go!' says Adijah.

'But nothin' change,' says Grandpa. 'Nothin'. De same bilgey water, de same cane trash burnin' and de same screamin' and yellin' from children.' He smiles eloquently and I can see that he is fully committed to the idea of coming home.

The day moves swiftly into the afternoon. We have been driving for about two hours. The sun had bared its head and now has begun to hide it. The muted colours of evening appear like bruises in the sky and then deepen into reds and crimsons. Then suddenly Picktown comes into view.

It is alive with expectation. Everywhere there seems to be a holiday atmosphere, with drums throbbing and people standing in clusters to see us. A banner across the road reads 'Welcome Home, Friends, Welcome to Picktown'.

'Why Picktown?' I ask Grandpa.

'Once upon a time you could pick any fruit by bagful in dis village. All you need do was bury a seed and wait to pick, pick, pick up de fruit.'

'Then dey was God's Mercy,' Grandma chimes in. 'Nothin' grow in dat place. One time a lot of people starve to death. One day you and Adijah must go see it. Really stony place, God's Mercy.'

People peer at us from doorways and windows. Nobody speaks. It is like an anthem of waiting voices.

The bungalow we have rented stands with manicured lawns and well-pruned shrubs in its own grounds. It must have been the home of fastidious people. The front of the house is almost hidden by a flamboyant tree in flower and with a seat like a handcuff around the trunk. Grandma scratches her head with one hand and points with the other. 'My house near here. Near to dis conversation tree,' she says. 'People use to meet up here after slavery day and discuss and give message. In slavery day dey call it Hangin' Tree. It where de runaway slaves meet dey maker. Our house use to be facin' dis tree. Over yonder.' She walks rapidly up to the tree.

102

'Conversation, I come back,' she says as if to a friend. 'You have t'ings to tell me – I have t'ings to tell you.'

Quietly she opens her bag, takes out the earth she has carried for so long, and pours it out close to the roots.

Relatives have come from far and near to welcome us. They are a motley crew – too overcome by the pain of separation and reunion to talk to us. Several can only hug Grandma and cry. The oldest ones thank their creator that they have seen the day of our return, and then set about feeding us. Each household has provided a dish and the quantity and variety of food are staggering. I cannot eat much and no amount of pleading can make me increase my appetite. As we prepare for bed, I notice that the windows are insect-proof and we do not need the insect repellants and ointments we have brought.

After a night of fitful sleep I am awakened by the persistent braying of donkeys and the doleful crowing of cockerels or fowl-cocks. They seem to be competing for the title of night-nuisance. The sun is already beaming down and the sunshine that floods our room is as bright as new gold. It is a truly tropical day, sparkling and breezy with the trees clear against the sky.

Going outdoors, I pick my first orange, but before I can eat it I notice a rather plump, oldish woman coming up the drive. She carries the largest basket of fruit I have ever seen. Part of her head and even her eyes appear to have lost themselves in the load she carries. I run towards her intending to help her, but she motions me away and continues towards the kitchen. 'I am Carrie, Auntie Carrie,' she says. 'Simon is my brother. I live up river. It take three day to get here.'

The reunion of Grandpa and the younger of his two 'ugly sisters' is something to see. They laugh, weep and talk. After a few minutes they talk, weep and laugh and talk again. She gives news of everyone – many have died, but just as many are alive. Grandpa and Grandma sit quietly, one on each side of Carrie, arms intertwined, all the harsh comments of the album forgotten. From time to time they cry and just as easily they laugh. Then we all eat breakfast. She stays with us for a few days then she goes back to her farm and her flock.

Adijah and I explore the extensive grounds, watching the hummingbirds use their needle-beaks to probe the flowers, the dragonflies hunting with their bunched-up, basket-like legs, and the ants focusing all their energies on the wealth of debris around us. Adijah is hypnotised by the precision with which the ants work.

'It makes me realise how unnecessary it is to use words to communicate,' she says. 'Just look at them!' Our world is dominant but under every bush and leaf there are other worlds where there is industry without argument and an application without distraction.

My grandparents join us in the garden. What a contrast they are to the fumbling, confused couple that resided at The Birches. They have found other strands of security. They have come home.

As the days pass Grandpa begins hook-and-line, sweet-water fishing with Big Mal, a friend of his youth. Grandma too is slowly becoming reacquainted with the Church Guilds. It does not matter if she walks slowly, talks slowly or repeats or forgets her words. The people about her accept old age and its handicaps. They measure persons against life rather than against youth. In Britain the young alone matter and elderly people are regarded as used-up and intractable simply because they are old. Long before Grandpa retired, he feared encounters with young black people in London streets – so aggressive and confrontational they seemed to be!

So I am not surprised when my grandparents decide to hold a soirée for their friends. They have taken the initiative and I am happy for them. But I don't know what to expect. I am still haunted by The Birches where time rendered people so helpless that they could only wait for the end.

When the day of the gathering arrives I am nervous from excitement and, had it not been for Adijah's good sense, I would have made myself quite ill with worry. Questions continue to plague me. What will the guests be like? How will they act? Will they be yesterday's people? My idea of yesterday was formed in a throwaway society. I too believe that people could become worthless and useless. I too do not always discriminate. I too am either defending my ground or attacking oppression!

They come, fifteen of them, six men and nine women. Yesterday's people they certainly are, but alert and able. One woman is led by her grandchildren because of the cataract in her eye. Another comes in a self-propelled wheelchair. Daddy Mac, a correct, precise old gentleman, is in fine form. 'I ent as active as befo',' he says. 'But at eighty-something a man slow down.' Many of these old folk have never retired and have stopped working only when their body-clocks bade them stop. They eat and drink and tell their stories with warmth and humour. A few fall asleep in the midst of things, but then Grandma says, 'Play you flute, Mac. You was a sweet flute player in you young days. You in the album, you know?'

Daddy Mac does not hesitate. He has come prepared to play and so after gently unwrapping his flute and carefully fixing the parts together, he plays 'Oh God Our Help in Ages Past', which they all sing, humbly and from the wellsprings of deep belief.

Then Grandpa says, 'Break away, Mac, flourish de flute. You was a real "flourish man" days gone by.'

Mac does break away, his fingers scurrying over the notes like ants over earth. Eyes tightly closed, he plays some of the most astonishing improvisations I have ever heard.

'Gosh,' says Adijah, 'that old man is cool!'

Too soon Mac's breathing forces him to stop playing.

'Don't stop, Mac,' yells Joe Congo, an old song and dance man, as he holds up a light aluminium crutch. 'All I lost is a foot and it never stop me dancing. See me.' And he dances until Mac stops playing again.

The music revitalises all of them and they talk into the twilight when one by one they are taken home by relatives. I can see my grandparents living on and on into the future. I wish that the Matron could hear them now especially when Grandma tells them the humorous story of Buru Ananse – the spider man evicted from his hole. She acts it, dances, dips and turns and so gets the hidden fear out of her system.

105

'It's the only way she could cope with the trauma of the racists and the car,' Adijah observes. 'They're really enjoying life here.'

I nod in agreement. 'They're going to live till they're eighty or ninety-something.'

We both laugh. The Islanders never number their years. 'Something' is used to denote any number between one and nine.

My parents too have grasped Island life with both hands. My father spends hours talking politics with his friends and Mum finds the role of the village hostess much more pleasurable than that of a working wife in rough, mugger-hugging west London. Mum has 'Been-to' England and the 'Been-tos' have one over on the 'Never-beens'. The 'Been-tos' could pretend to 'missyfied'.

This becomes as clear as spring water after an invitation to open the Whitsun Fair reaches my mother. It is sent by the Women's Guild, who previously offered such honours to white officials or to members of the various overseas aid agencies that sometimes stopped 'for a chat' in Picktown. My mother clucks relentlessly over the recognition she has been shown while my father yawns with the weariness of all that talk.

On the day of the fête, closeted with Adijah, my mother spends hours trying to conceal the time-cracks and age-scars on her face, and arranging her hair in a suitably spectacular design. Laughter is thrown around the room like balls in the hands of excited children, and the obvious pleasure the women show as they bite into grapes and Californian apples leads me to conclude that they are simply being self-conscious over their efforts to dress like true Island women. Imagine my surprise at the sight of them rigged out as for a tea party in London on an uncertain summer's day.

'You two going up Buck House to see the Queen?' I sneer. 'We didn't bring any flags, you know!'

My mother tries to scalp me with her eyes but Adijah says nothing. She simply flicks a recalcitrant eyelash from her dress and adds more lipstick to the mask she has already made of her face. We drive in silence to the venue where a sizeable and colourful crowd waits. My mother is now steeped in feelings of self-importance, and I listen dispiritedly as she makes her speech in the voice she keeps for special occasions. I notice that like a growing amphibian, she has begun to change in a way that I can never accept. She dances with the enigmatic vicar and I dance with Adijah but the spirit of the dance is no longer with me.

The eyes of the young people almost perforate us with resentment that can be felt like heat against the body and for the first time in this long saga of events I cannot aptly describe my feelings. The steel band suddenly stops. Everyone claps. It is then that I notice my mother's little white gloves that in my opinion set her apart.

I am none the less happy to see my parents swept into the main stream of village life. And then by chance Adijah and I wander into the Pickville Hotel and find my mother having lunch with Cookson Tollgate, the local solicitor whom everyone calls 'Cookie'. He is the vainest and most self-important lecher I have ever had the misfortune to know. He is a hearty man, easily familiar with his clients, and thinks of himself as God's gift to women on account of his profession alone. He has acted as our solicitor. Looking at him, I always feel that at some crucial stage of his development someone had smacked him across the face with a large fillet of fish. When I see him with Mum he is so close to her I think that he is the mother bird, she is the fledgling and it is feeding time.

'Hi, Mum,' I say.

'Hi, Mum,' Adijah echoes.

'Hi, Mr Tollgate! Hi, Cookie!' we add.

'Ah, yes, Tyrone.' Cookie beams. 'I just giving your mum some professional advice. You want listen?'

'Oh no, Cookie. You tell Mum. Then she will tell my dad and he will tell your wife.'

'Ah, yes. I see what you saying. I better go.'

We both laugh. Mum looks sternly into her plate.

Adijah makes a face. I hug her.

'Mum,' I whisper. 'What you don't do in London, don't do here. He's worse than Dad. Dad has asthma and principles.'

At supper that evening Goldberg's name surfaces. We'd forgotten about him and a heated argument as to whose fault it is develops. Grandpa objects to the fact that we have all got selfish and are all too busy 'to put him down properly'. Mum and Dad leave the room in shame but return soon after and contritely give us a date for the wake and the iterment. When she collected Goldberg's urn and ashes from Mama Kane, my mother had remonstrated with herself for leaving it so long. She now decides that to make up for her neglect Goldberg will have a lovely wake and 'a really wonderful burying'.

For days they bake bread and cakes, prepare meats and fruit and decorate the house with leaves and flowers to symbolise Goldberg's youth at the time of death. The priest supervises the dressing of the church in white and blue flowers and the coffin-maker polishes the coffin till it shines like burnished metal. On the night of the wake it rains, and the hymns are chosen to raise the spirits of those who brave the weather. Food and drink compete in quantity with the water from the heavens. A blind-drunk relative explains that the rain means that Goldberg is mourning for his youth, and then suddenly slumps down on the floor, argues briefly with himself and snores.

On the whole young people avoid me. I resemble them and yet am not of their world – neither speaking nor behaving like them. They have heard about the awkwardness of London-born blacks, of our disrespect, of our disregard for authority. They lump us all together. To them I am a London black. A weird species of humanity – probably glad that my brother had died.

Later that evening it strikes me that no one knows or cares who Goldberg was. They have come in search of food and drink and a comfortable place to sit down. When they wail, it is for the discomfort caused by their overeating and their greed. But Grandpa and Grandma call everyone to silence and talk of the virtues of my brother, and it is comforting for us all to think of him for a few moments in our new, comfortable and busy life. The interment is also simple. We are all suitably dressed and receive our condolences, sincerely meant, with graciousness and humility. Time has passed but that matters little. Our grief is new and as fresh as ever.

The grave has been dug in the 'Grainger plot' and everyone

praises the grave-digger for the neatness and precision with which he has worked. He even had the foresight to protect the grave from the rain, covering it with sheets of corrugated iron.

Afterwards Grandma leads us down winding, leaf-strewn paths to her parents' grave. We are having a conducted tour round the gardens of the dead. Here ancestors matter, and their final resting places are kept neat and tidy to await the trumpet sound and the resurrection.

'Talk to you great-grandpa and ma, Tyrone,' my Grandma orders.

'What should I say, Grandma? I don't even know them. Their names or anything.'

'Dey is family,' says Grandpa. 'You believe in family. You don't have to know. I do it for you so you learn for you and your childrun.'

I nod.

'Mama and Papa,' he says reverently. 'We all standin' here. Me, my wife Clara and my grandson and his girl. Bless us and keep us till we join you in heaven after showin' de young people de right road. We was in a home for old, but de Lord help us get out and we never say about dat. It is a shame on us so forgive us. Amen.'

'Say the Amen, Tyrone,' urges Grandma. 'It good for you. You always walk wid us. You always like de fillin' in de sandwich. We put goodness and Christian love inside you like food.'

'Amen,' I comply. I have been their agent all along. This is the last time. We walk home not daring to speak lest we break the spell of 'properness' that has come over my grandparents. They are suddenly aware of their subsequent mortality and of their present respectability.

After the funeral it is giveaway time. Relatives I have never seen before unashamedly ask for some of our possessions – clothes, shoes, anything. My mother throws herself into being a source of supplies and when I see my clothes disappearing, I feel compelled to ask her whether she intends sending me back to London parcelled up in newspaper.

Grandpa and Grandma sit silently turning the pages of the

album. They sit close, their forms aflame with memory and without any sadness that I can observe. Only the glow of happiness shines in their faces. At last Grandma speaks. 'My Grandpa Vanette did not give us much food. I want him to see we got food to give away to poor people. Do you t'ink his spirit can see us?'

'He can see, Grandma,' I whisper. 'He can see. He knows you're sharing what you have. You're a good woman!'

We go out each day to look around Picktown. People invite us into their homes. TV aerials protruding from corrugated-iron roofs bring distant places to view and it is not unusual to see people clustered around the sets watching and envying the rich amid the poverty of their hovels. Do these poor people appreciate the workings of the affluent society? We pass by the church. The priest sits alone. He is slowly becoming a displaced person. By the turn of a knob the TV evangelists can come right into the home of his flock and make his ministry redundant. Does he, do they understand the nature of the change that has almost come to them?

It is late when we return home. The night is full of sounds - all the sounds of a warm tropical night. Adijah sits beside me. I feel her body relaxed and soft. The contentment inside her could be squeezed out like juice from a fruit. But within myself I feel the resonance of some unspoken need. It isn't my desire to read or my love of books; nor do I miss the press and indifference of people. I conclude that it is my need for anonymity. In London I am of no particular importance to anyone. I am unknown except to my family and friends. I have grown up with just an urban identity and come to cherish that. In Picktown I am trapped – in my family identity, the identity of my community and the identity of my opportunity. In London I had lived another life, grown other feelings, got to know myself as 'Tyrone'. I know how and where I am vulnerable. I understand my difference. As long as I live at home I will always be part of Grandma, Grandpa, Mum, Dad, the community, the Church. I cannot handle becoming the Picktown person. I do not want the involvement of 'belonging' without the choice of 'not belonging'. I feel unhappy

110

outside my harsh urban skin, unable to site myself in time and space.

'Face it, Tyrone, you've done a lot,' consoles my mother. 'When you go to Cambridge it will be better.'

'I'm not going to Cambridge,' I say.

'What you mean, you not goin'? What you mean by dat?' demands my father, bloating his face like a bullfrog, anger undermining his careful English speech. 'You get opportunity people give the right eye for and all you say is "I'm not goin'"'. You tantalisin' us? You is a prima donna? All dat work – all our hopes down de drain for nothing?'

'No,' I say. 'But I prefer to go to Howard University. A black one. I don't feel the need to be pseudo white, pseudo British or pseudo black. I don't want to be a token black swanning around up there.'

'But Cambridge is the best,' shout both my parents.

'The best!' I say sarcastically. 'Here people compete to have the best latrines. Mum, you don't know!' I emphasise *know*. Several clichés about knowing run wildly through my head. I know too that I will have to go to Cambridge, whatever I say.

Adijah titters. 'Don't worry, Robby,' she says. 'Tyrone is the master of cut and thrust.'

'Oh, God,' I almost roar. 'Not you as well. Give me some support. Give me my space. Reclaim it for me! Help me!'

'I want my own space,' she shouts back.

I go into the bedroom and pace around like a caged tiger ready to pounce but Adijah does not come. Later I hear them going through the door.

'We're off to the Pickville for a quiet supper, Tyrone. Want to come?' a voice calls to me. They are the pseudo whites now! Resentment burns inside me like acid.

I wake early. The house is quiet. Adijah sleeps soundly so I get up, shower and dress. I feel isolated and the anger inside me is still simmering. Why won't they believe me? Why won't they stop treating me as if I do not know for myself? I look in on my grandparents. They too are asleep. The day is bright as a brass button and open-legged outside. On the grass the dewlets shine like tiny clusters of glass beads but I can still feel anger and resentment like two lumps of rock weighing me down. I decide to go to Widow's-Dip and maybe swim out to sea with my pocket full of stones. I'll take my camera just in case I decide against it.

As soon as I open the door Adijah stirs. She is talking in her sleep, or pretending to.

'Oh, Cookie,' she is saying. 'You're so strong – so romantic.' She purses her lips and kisses the air half a dozen times. 'Oh, Cookie, you fan the flames of my heart.' I can hear her giggling into the pillow. It is her sense of fun again!

As I walk on I wish I were back in London and could find a pub. I would sit outside my favourite, the Swan and Pyramid, and wait until it opened and play a furious game of darts to clear my system. Grandpa had told me how they had fought to secure entry to pubs but they have always been open to me. I find the rum shops strange and different. I am unable to settle in them with the smell of rum for company. I let my imagination float as one by one I recall the names of the pubs I had visited in London on my eighteenth birthday. I chuckle to myself. It is a beautiful memory – young and drunk and pub-crawling at eighteen! No wonder I've never done it since.

'Chu, man! Big time!' I shout to no one in particular.

'Whoops.' I wiggle to the tunes that have crept into my brain, jump high into the air and run on down the road.

CHAPTER THIRTEEN

I continue along the road which is like most people – asleep. Cats and dogs that have been hunting and carousing through the night are slowly going home. An old woman, clucking like a tired-out mother hen, feeds her chicks handfuls of corn. Another supervises a few browsing lambs.

Widow's-Dip is a pretty place – a little cove nibbled in the side of the Island by the sea and then surrounded by mounds of tufty sand-grass and beds of tiny yellow flowers, slightly larger than buttercups. I sit in the shade watching nature. Time passes. The day grows older.

I notice Stephy in the distance out of the corner of my eye. She is a cousin twice removed. Cousins once removed are called 'brothers and sisters' in the islands. Everybody seems to know and rely on Stephy, and of all the young girls I have met she is one of the few that does not have a child clinging to her. Always neat and tidy, every strand of hair in place, she is very correct in her behaviour. It is as if, like a good strategist, every move is planned. But sometimes she seems a quietly sleeping volcano biding her time. And then there are those days I think of as her market days. As she watches, as she participates in the village happenings, those oval-shaped and clear brown eyes are buyer's eyes, closely examining what is on offer at the stalls of life. Only her fingertips touch the things she likes until she is ready to snatch. Even if she has no money for her purchases, she will always find a way to get the pick of the bunch.

The heat of the sun is still mild enough to be enervating and, aware of Stephy's presence, I let my mind revisit London, while

I wait for her to make her move. On the sand opposite the crabs sidle away as small chicken-hawks hover close.

'Hello, Tyrone. What you doing here? It's just past day-dawn.'

'And you, Stephy. I can ask the same.'

'I see you pass my door. I follow you. I make it nearly eight.'

'Nice, clean morning. Come sit down.' She sits down.

'How do you find living here? Don't you want more than this?' I quiz.

'I trying to go to America. I have a brother there but the sponsoring take a long time. I have to wait and see.'

'Are you in the Party?'

'Yes, you have to. But you know what that mean? First they own you and then they really own you. I keep away.'

'What do you do for sport? For pleasure?'

'We play rounders and go once a month to disco in the town. There is a US base near here. Sometimes I go to their dance. You know how to dance soca? Picktown soca?'

'I like Picktown. It's a quiet place, soca or no soca.'

The lie nearly singes my tongue.

'Every man to his own. I born here, I want to go from here. Home is for when you young and when you old. In between you go and grow somewhere else. Where's Adijah? You not often alone.'

'She don't like it too hot. She was in a fire.'

'Yes, we see it on TV. Twelve people – young people – burn!'

'She was playing music there. She jumped. It was touch and go for her.'

She feels sorry. I can see. She nestles beside me. She is feeling flames – mine and hers.

'You like hot sun? It soon get hot,' she says dreamily.

We lie there, two curious young people sharing a need, the need for home, facing the need to escape from home. I kiss her tentatively. She does not kiss me back. She just accepts it. There is no dissent. No discord. She accepts me totally. There are no words, just harmony and then ecstasy. She is delightfully receptive to me. I lie there enjoying the after-glow – riding high but suddenly she springs up, dusts herself and disappears as she had come. A crack of twigs. A whiff of the scent Adijah has given her. I can see that she feels conquered – yet again.

I hear the hidden despair in her receding footsteps and then there is silence. Momentarily my sense of maleness ebbs and flows in all its power and then I too feel stigmatised and guilty. In reality I should be experiencing a powerful feeling of conquest. Stephy is special and she has not repulsed me. I am Tyrone Grainger, another Island rake in the making. Suddenly the whole enterprise of coming home turns into a farce. The Island seems a confused mess. The longer I stay the more frequent such acts of betrayal would become and more and more young women seeking a way out of the press of their circumstances would yield to my demands. 'Cookie' flashes like neon lights before me. I am becoming a bit like him. The way I look at the young girls I pass, my fantasies out of control!

I feel a sharp change culminating in a hatred for the Island. Grandpa's, Grandma's, my parents'. Their Island. I hate the way it shuts me in, and the sloth-like passage of time that lulls me into a false sense of ease and insensibility. I hate the betrayal of young people and the very many illiteracies about black Londoners like me. Most of all I hate my misunderstanding of the idea of home. I don't belong here. And this morning, with the murmuring waters and racing clouds in the distance, I know it. I am British and believe it. I too scramble up to a new realisation. I dust myself and walk resolutely home. I want to call myself British for the first time in my life.

Adijah sits eating her breakfast in the garden, and fussing about the flies and other tiny creatures that see fit to offend her. Flecks of sunshine break through the leaves and pattern her hair while butterflies settle on the nearby hibiscus flowers. She has become an Island girl, at ease amongst the sunshine, the pineapples, the melons, the insects and the flowers. Sensing something, her eyes question me. I smile and say flatly, 'I am going home.'

'Home,' she sneers as she bites into a crescent of watermelon, gulping down both flesh and juice while ejecting the beetle-black

115

seeds on to the ground. 'What kind of insult is that? Your home is here – isn't it?'

'I am going home,' I say again. Only in a flatter tone and with more resolution. 'I am going back to England.'

She ignores me. It is as if her ears are just decorations on her head. I repeat myself. Still she ignores me. I can see that her lips are set, and her eyes as hard and as stubborn as her mood. I go upstairs to think. The money has been amicably sorted out and there is no anger or discontent between my family and myself. Everyone has been agreeable to the three-way split.

Outside, the breakfast game of dominoes is in full swing, with Big Mal in his element and chortling at the possibility of a win over my grandparents. In the distance on the wide brown-burnt grass, Stephy plays with her dog. I go back to Adijah, angry that she is winding me up by ignoring me.

'This is no joke, Adijah,' I say quietly. 'I am going. Don't play games. This is a serious time for us. You had better stop and listen.'

'What did you say?' she asks, mixing menace with spite in her voice. I repeat myself.

'Take me seriously, I'm going back . . .'

Before I can finish she screams, 'Shut bloody up!' as if she has been attacked by a swarm of those little wasps which nest in the shrubs growing by the roadside. Marabuntas, the Island people call them. There are torrents of tears, sobs and more scatological language that would make the devil blush if such a thing were at all possible.

My father rushes out to us. 'No need for such language, Adijah, in my home. Who is going where?' She points to me. Since her accident she has become 'hair trigger' and waspish but my parents always ignore her outbursts.

She sobs, 'He is not touring as we planned. He's going back, to the racism, the dole and the National Front – the dirt and the despair. Remember the eviction?'

'And the unemployment, the grime, the history and your university – King's College,' I say. 'Some go back now, some later.'

116

She then remembers that she is expected to return as well and a bewildered look overruns her face.

'I am going back to what I understand and can deal with.' I speak more softly after my point has been made.

There is now a tight knot of family surrounding me. They are strangling me with the closeness of their presence. My grandmother, the tears shining like daubed glycerine on her face, feels let down. Like my grandfather she sees me as a fixture, a part of their conscious mental life; but I have failed my father yet again. This time I am going away. 'Away' means distance although he has 'gone away' himself in more ways than one.

'Stop talking foolish,' he says, a milky note in his voice. 'Why're you going back to England? It's a third world country. A bit more up-class than this but still third world. And one is as good as another. Besides, it's always warm here. And is always cool-time. No bustling. No fussing. Everything's cool.' He sniggers like a teenager. It doesn't suit him one little bit. His age is showing.

My mother goes on about never knowing where I would jump next. She recounts all my stupidities from the time I was born. I suck my teeth sneakily to show my anger at the attack upon my whole mode of being in this world. But Adijah hears me. 'Don't suck your teeth at your mother!' she yells. 'You pompous twit. No respect for parents! No nothing! You're not too big for a cuff from your mother. Round your thick ears!'

'Look,' I say, throwing up my hands. 'There's nothing here for me to think about or feel other than helpless about. There's only boredom, stagnation and deviousness here, and you're becoming a cantankerous bully.'

'Who stop you from thinking?' my mother yells. 'People with brains think anywhere – everywhere – all the time! They don't get bored. They don't stagnate.'

'Since he sold that picture he fancies himself as a financier. He's nothing but a huckster.'

Adijah seems suddenly overcome by her own behaviour and by her own loss of control.

117

'This is home, Tyrone!' Grandma coaxes in an effort to console and reconcile.

'It is our home,' Grandpa says. 'But it is not Tyrone home. London is what he know. He must not sleep wid our eyes.'

Grandpa is the only one trying hard not to emasculate me. I remember him quietly telling me how gangs of racists used to surround the house in which he lived, effectively stopping his mates from going to work and the night-shift workers from going indoors to sleep. He alone knows what I feel with loving anti-racists around me like garish wrapping paper.

'How can he go back? Yes, how can he go back? He is not used to suffering on his own.'

Their voices rise and fall in unison, in counterpoint.

I listen wearily. They must leave me to decide and act on my own, for myself. I must shape my life without interference. I must grow and achieve for myself alone. Not by being pushed from behind by four pairs of pernicketty, meddlesome hands. I have done as I said. I have chosen to look out for my grandparents and that has been accomplished without regret.

'Everybody is getting out of England and you are rushing in where angels fear.' Adijah uses her voice like a jagged knife when it suits her.

'People are risking their lives to get there,' I reply calmly. 'Think before you talk, Adijah. Besides, your family is doing rather nicely, moonlighting on the dole!'

'Leave my family out. My father is retired. My brother pays his taxes.'

'I'm sure he does,' I reply pointedly. 'Now and then.'

For years, four years in fact, my heart has ached and longed for Adijah. I have loved her, but now she attacks me with cruel words and drains me of all good feelings about myself. Not daring to turn my back on her, I edge out of the room and begin to collect my things. There is more than sentiment at stake. My manhood itself is on the line. The tempo of my packing increases under pressure from my mind. A few books, a few shirts, changes of socks and underwear. I am soon ready to leave. I can feel anger shredding my insides like some strangely determined machine.

I peck Adijah on the cheek and she freezes at my touch. She has become someone else, taken on a whole new personality. One I cannot entertain. She has suddenly changed not only all the rules of our game, but all her expectations.

'Finish your holiday,' I whisper. 'Let our love breathe. We are strangling it to death with what we are learning about ourselves. The one emotion that I have felt every day is anger. I have been angry for months. That can't be good for me. I must get away.'

My mum also stiffens at my touch. 'After the dark comes the dawn,' I tease. 'The sun will shine as hard as ever tomorrow. Nothing will change. You'll see. Both Dad and Cookie will be there. I promise.' A brief smile flits across her face but the stoneyness lingers like a wind-waxed flame.

'Goodbye, Grandma.' A series of rapid nods from her and then tears.

'I'll miss you, Tyrone. You been good to me,' she sobs.

'Follow you heart,' says Grandpa, 'and you star. You was wid us at every dip and turn of our long, weary road.'

'This is all there is, Grandpa,' I say. 'All that I could give! My breast has run dry. It's time for weaning. You said yourself. Sometimes hot-pepper and bitters must be used at weaning-time.'

'I'll drive you to the airport,' my father volunteers. I cannot help noticing how much more robust in spirit he has become with the passing of the months. 'If you're going you might as well be gone,' he adds, jangling his car keys. As we climb into the car I can almost reach out and touch the effort with which he controls himself. Big Mal waves from the drawing-room window. I have forgotten all about him and throughout the argument he has sat waiting, with just the dominoes for company.

My father drives straight ahead, steers straight ahead, unsmilingly. At last I say, 'I'll be back, Dad. Going now is important.' The journey continues in a suffocating, searing silence. When at last we say goodbye I can sense the threat in his hand-shake. I watch him drive away and momentarily think about his asthma. Suddenly he leans out of the window and waves to me. He has set me free.

If I hurry I'll be just in time to start my course. I can hear Grandpa saying in his sensible biblical way, 'Better de devil you know to de devil you don't'.

CHAPTER FOURTEEN

I sit contemplatively over a Coca Cola as I wait for the flight call with a battle of loyalties raging inside me. Adijah moves through the battlefield like a drummer, thumping out her learned rhythms. Then the truce comes and the seasons return. Not the wet–dry seasons of the tropics. But the seasons I have always known. I think of winter and of the remarkable way in which it transformed our local park into a wonderland of cut-crystal, and how once long ago the trees behind Grandma's house were turned into a fairyland sculptured in frost and ice. I think too of my walk past the pond in spring, where the ice crackled and released God's tiny creatures. The trees would slyly show leaf and the lengthening days mysteriously bring abundance, abundance of flowers, leaves and fruit, until autumn once again appeared with its gifts of colours and clever designs of cloud, sky and sea. I become aware of myself in that place, at that time. I am at the mercy of a love that will not let me go.

I stand among the fragments of conversation and the inquisitive glances of passers-by. I can feel myself shedding my anger, shedding my frustrations. My thoughts pirouette and then stop upon Adijah yet again. I have known and loved her for so long. She has been all that love has meant to me. All that I could know of love. But she has gone in a flash. Of course we have made a relationship, discovered some of life's turnings, played at being wed, talked of our undying love and played games with each other's emotions. We are too young. We only play at loving. Such are my thoughts. For a moment I am sad at the loss of all that we have shared; and then there is an explosion inside me. I feel happy. I believe now and always will that our experiences together and with others have not been wasted. I am at last on my own.

When I settle into my seat, the anxiety of take-off vanishes. The old, white couple beside me ignores me. I thumb through a copy of *Dylan Thomas in America*, circa 1956, which someone has fortuitously forgotten.

The non-smoking area is sparsely occupied: a few elderly women returning to London and its environs, a few younger women, one with a gurgling baby, and me. Between yawns I think of my people, and of the illusionary journey I have undertaken to what is called home.

Some of the women on the plane stealthily smile at me. Others read the magazines wet-ragged from use. After a few minutes, boredom chokes any friendship that might have sprouted amongst us. We stop at a neighbouring island for numerous passengers all going away from their reality.

From the back of the plane, however, the young island-men in a large, colourful group are the true kings of the moment. Laughter ruptures the pall of cigarette smoke that hangs about them. I can see the hope in their actions and in their eyes. They are, so they think, leaving all their shackles and frustrations behind them. They have not yet realised that those shackles and frustrations will take on new shapes and new forms in a society that will reinterpret what is different about them. These young men also are leaving on the same quest as my grandfather nearly forty years before. They share the same dreams of fortunes, castles and queens and of offspring in various numbers and ages; offspring who will one day return to the Island and find that coming home is not a panacea but a service for old folk seeking a familiar graveyard.